A *LOWRY* TO *DIE* FOR

A novel by
THOMAS GLASER

ASHRIDGE PRESS

Published and distributed by:
Ashridge Press
A subisdiary of Country Books
Courtyard Cottage, Little Longstone, Bakewell, Derbyshire DE45 1NN
Tel/Fax: 01629 640670
e-mail: dickrichardson@country-books.co.uk

ISBN 1 901214 22 2

British Library Cataloguing in Publication Data.
A catalogue record for this book is available from the British Library.

This book creatively combines fact with fiction.
Although most events are based on fact,
others are figments of the author's imagination.

Cover Picture:
Reproduction of *Mill Gates* by kind permission of the Lowry Estate.

Printed and bound by:
Antony Rowe Ltd.

FOREWORD

I promised Nathan long, long ago, when we were young men that I would do this – set down his story and my own.

"When you get to my part, make me a little taller and a whole lot better looking," he instructed, his brown eyes twinkling with amusement, "And put down how Great Art saved my life."

Ironically, if Great Art saved his life, it also took it from him. For now my friend is gone, and nothing remains but paintings and memories of the past.

It's with a heavy heart that I sit down in my study, pull out from the drawer the dusty old diaries and try, at last, to keep my word...

TOM'S STORY

CHAPTER 1

Berlin, June 1939.

After making love, we crawled out of the secluded love-nest we had made in the shrubbery. We stood up. I brushed the leaves from Gisela's hair. As far as I was concerned, she was the most beautiful girl in the world. Already fully formed, she had blondish wavy hair that she wore loose around her shoulders, blue eyes that reacted to everything I said and a sensuous mouth. We had been meeting there most days since May, having discovered the spot by accident whilst on a country walk. She was fifteen also. We were in the same class at school. It was a friendship fraught with danger.

"Go through the back streets, Thomas," she said, "don't take any chances." She kissed me on the cheek, "Until tomorrow."

We always made our way home separately to avoid being seen together. I watched her leave and the countdown to tomorrow's meeting began. By early evening there was more of the enemy about, and I needed to be careful. Twice I did an about turn, since I didn't like what I saw ahead; but I made it safely, as I always did, to our home at 27, Tauntzien Strasse in the centre of town.

We had two floors in that austere building, divided between my father's practice and our spacious living accommodation. The moment I entered, I knew that something big was afoot. There was a distinct air of foreboding. My mother had clearly been crying, and the fact that my father was wearing his pince-nez was an indication of serious business.

My mother's sister, Auntie Gerda was there with her husband Ludwig, as well as my father's sister, Auntie Matilde. The two aunties were not on good terms and there had to be a very good reason for them to be under the same roof, let alone in the same room and at the same table. They were seated in such a way that eye contact could be avoided.

My brother Paul was next to my mother. He had just turned eighteen and took great pride in his appearance. Today was no exception; he wore an elegant suit, in the top pocket of which he sported a navy and white check handkerchief that matched his tie. His black hair was slicked with a touch of Brilliantine. I often thought that the good Lord had distributed all the brain-power and good looks in his direction at my expense. He was already at University reading medicine, in readiness to join the family practice. I always felt and looked shabby beside him. He was all the things that I was not. In retrospect, I see that this took the pressure off me, which was not a bad thing.

Ellen, the last remaining servant, had laid an impressive tea-table with a selection of sandwiches and home-made cakes. The best china was in evidence. I hadn't eaten since breakfast. My mother picked a good selection of the sandwiches and cakes, which she knew I liked best, and placed an over-full plate in front of me.

My father addressed me directly, "It's just as well you're here, Thomas, because what we have been talking about concerns you and Paul." He cleared his throat. "This morning I have had a decree that my practice will be closed down. So now it is the professional people who are being persecuted. The position is bad enough now, but it will get worse before it gets better."

My mother, impatient to get to the point, broke in, "Leo, tell the boys about the train."

He gave her a stern look. "I am coming to that Marga, all in good time." He turned his eyes back to us; "I hear reports, through the profession, that there are camps of some sort in which the regime is so hard and food so scarce that people are dying of overwork and starvation. It will only be a question of time before our turn comes. We have no alternative but to pack up and leave the country while we still can. We are trying to get an exit visa for all of us, and immigration papers to England or America. The American consulate says they have no quota available. It could take time, perhaps six months. Have we got that long? We have to hope we do."

6

At this point he became too emotional to continue, and drew his handkerchief from his trouser pocket to wipe his eyes.

Mother took over, "The Rabbis have got together and negotiated a deal with the Nazis. All children under the age of seventeen have a free pass to leave the country and go to England. Special carriages will be reserved on regular trains and, when you get there, they will look after you in homes, staying with a family. We hear that the trains will soon be stopped. So your father and I have put your names down. I have already paid the deposit of fifty pounds for each of you. You will take the train tomorrow."

Paul and I looked at each other in dismay. Neither of us wanted to leave, though for different reasons.

"Once you are safe," she went on, "We will all of us here do everything possible to leave the country and join you. On the other hand, if things settle down here, and it becomes safe to come back, then that is what we will do. One way or the other, we will be apart for only a short time."

The two aunties, in agreement for once, nodded approval.

"How difficult will it be for us to get out?" asked Mathilde.

Mother said: "If we have to, we will buy our passage out. We have money."

Paul was first to raise an objection. "Did you not say, Mother, that the age limit was seventeen? I am now eighteen and two months."

"I altered your birth Certificate to 1922," she replied, "It's quite easy to turn a one into a two. No one will detect the change, so now it's only two months over. No one will notice."

I was full of misgivings. Paul looked very mature for his years. He had been shaving for some time and was swarthy. To my eyes, he looked nearer twenty than seventeen. I cried a little, protesting that it was wrong to split the family. Should we not stay together? I felt very unhappy to be leaving my parents. But mother declared firmly that, horrible though it was to split up, it was the right thing for us boys, at least, to be safe and out of harm's way.

I had a sinking feeling in my stomach as all objections were overruled.

How could I leave my beloved Gisela? Worse, I couldn't even see her to say 'goodbye', nor even be able to tell her what was happening. I pictured her sitting on the rug in our hiding place and waiting…. and waiting. The thought was too terrible.

My mother put both arms around me, "Don't cry, my darling Thomas. We'll soon be back together."

CHAPTER 2

The Kindertransport was due to leave Berlin Hauptbahnhof at ten a.m. Two hours before departure, the first trickle of children began to arrive. They were of varying ages, accompanied by dour-faced parents and relatives. Most of the adults wore the yellow star, which made them vulnerable to harassment from over-zealous Nazis – as if seeing off their loved ones was not trauma enough.

At the station, we reported to our official escort. She carried a clipboard listing the names of all the 'Kinder'. Once she had ticked a name off the list, she issued a numbered brown luggage label, already completed with the name, address and age of each 'Kind'. It had a string attached, which was fastened to lapel or button, so as to be visible at all times.

We were each allowed one small suitcase of restricted dimensions. Mother had crammed, rather than packed, our cases, to ensure we had a change of clothing and woollies for the winter. There was also a letter written 'to whom it may concern', begging for love and care of her sons until their repatriation, and offering financial reward for safe delivery. In addition, we carried a shoulder bag, packed with food and drink that would see us through the journey and beyond.

Family groups were assembling in clusters on the platform, awaiting the train's arrival. Some of the youngsters knew each other. Their parents were heroically making small talk, trying to keep emotion at bay ahead of the final farewell. There were children of all ages. Little girls who could have been no older than three, accompanied by older brothers and sisters. Some, not understanding the solemnity of their exit, were excited at the prospect of a train journey.

Two Gestapo officers were milling amongst the crowd. Occasionally, they would stop to read a label to register name and age.

The older boys and girls, only too well aware of the circumstances, were sobbing, as were their parents.

I will never forget those last minutes we were together. My father was so emotional he could not utter a word. The tears just rolled down his cheeks. My mother, on the other hand, spoke incessantly, in a vain attempt to detach herself mentally from the farewell, relieving our gloom by assuring us time and again that we would be reunited within six months.

Just then, an official in black uniform took a close look at our identification labels. He seemed to be more interested in Paul's than mine. Having taken note, he moved on. I have to admit that Paul looked out of place with all the children. So grown up and tall, even though he had dressed casually for once, with open necked shirt and short trousers to make him look younger.

Nervously, I cast my eye around the assembled families. There must have been more than one hundred children. It was a sea of white hankies, an ocean of tears.

The train steamed and hissed its way noisily onto the platform. Two joined-up carriages were allocated to 'Kindertransport'.

After a final embrace, the 'Kinder' stampeded into the compartments to take up window seats. There were at least ten little faces peering out of each window to catch a last glimpse of weeping parents.

Paul and I waved until ours disappeared from view. I observed that my poor, dear mother had finally stopped talking and now clung to my father in a tearful embrace.

It is a memory I will take with me to the grave.

CHAPTER 3

As the steam train laboured on its way, we stared forlornly out of the rain-streaked window. Paul and I were sat opposite one another. We shared the carriage with four other boys. One of them was sobbing his heart out. I looked at his label. David Aaronson. Nine years old. He had a friendly face with a mop of unruly hair that covered his eyes. His front teeth were large and crooked. I placed a paternal arm around his shoulder, "Don't cry, David," I said, "I'll look after you. You'll be alright." David seemed to take comfort from my words, "Can I stay with you?" he asked, drying his eyes.

"Of course," I replied, "you're one of the family now."

This pleased him no end and a few minutes later he was smiling, colouring a book with crayons he pulled from his satchel.

Paul and I sat silent. After what we had been through, we were in no mood for conversation. We watched the Berlin suburbs thin out before making way for green fields and woodland. Sheep and cows were grazing peacefully in the summer drizzle.

For a time we travelled alongside the Autobahn – symbol of Hitler's progressive Germany. Some of the 'Kinder' waved as the train overtook speeding Mercedes and Opels.

Our carriages were littered with the refuse of previous 'Kinder'. Comics, books, crayons, banana skins, orange peel, half-eaten sandwiches now rancid. Bottles were on and under the seats and all the bins were filled to capacity. German cleanliness had clearly been set aside, and orders issued that the 'Kindertransport' carriages were not to be cleaned between journeys. This was confirmed when I made my first visit to the toilet. It was filthy and reeked of excreta. There was no lavatory paper. Handkerchiefs had been used and thrown away, and there was evidence of fingers wiped on walls. There was no water to flush or wash.

I returned to my seat, relieved to breathe fresh air. Little David asked where I had been. I told him about the toilet. He laughed.

I watched the countryside flash past, immersed in thought. Wild ideas were going through my head. How could I find a way of getting Gisela to England? My life without her was meaningless. I would write to her as soon as I had an address in England and bring her over. It was the only way I could contemplate my new life away from home. For one brief moment I smiled at the solution in the belief that I could make it happen. My reverie was interrupted sharply, when the communicating door between carriages was slid open.

The Gestapo officer in black uniform that we had seen on the platform stood over us. Gruffly he addressed Paul, "Your papers."

The colour had visibly drained from Paul's face as he presented the required documents.

The official looked at them, then him, then asked, "Your date of birth?"

Paul remained calm, remembered the lost year, "May 19th. 1922."

"You will stand when you speak to a German Officer. And you will call him 'Sir'. Do you understand me?"

"Yes Sir, I understand."

Obediently Paul rose. He was taller than the officer. I thought to myself, oh my God, he looks twenty-five, even with his short trousers.

"So what do you wish me to believe is your age today?"

"I am seventeen years and two months, Sir."

"Huh. You expect me to believe that, Schweinhund?"

"I assure you Sir, that is my age."

Enraged, the officer struck Paul with his open hand across the face,

"That's for your insolence."

The blow forced Paul to fall back into his seat. His face was badly bruised. The Officer roared at him, "I thought I told you to stand when speaking to an Officer."

Sheepishly Paul rose again. "I am sorry, Sir."

I had crazy thoughts racing through my mind. Should I creep up behind and hit him? Fortunately I couldn't see anything suitable to do it with. Conversation in the carriage had stopped. All eyes were on the confrontation.

The Gestapo Officer was now looking closely at the papers. He pulled a magnifying glass from the pocket of his jacket, held it to his eye and scrutinised the date of birth. Without hesitation he said, "I arrest you for forgery and lying to a German Officer. It is quite clear from the papers that your date of birth has been changed from 1921 to 1922. You will leave the train at Potsdam for further questioning."

Shaking, I rose and said, "Please, Sir, I need my brother to help me when I arrive. You see, Sir, I am not well and need my brothers' care." If questioned further, I'm sure I would have thought of something. But there was no need. The Officer showed no concern for my well being.

He mumbled under his breath, "So, one Jewboy less, who cares?" Out loud he said, "The Führer has ordered seventeen years, no older. You will leave the train at Potsdam. We arrive in five minutes."

I tried again, "I will leave the train also. My parents said we must stay together."

For answer, he pushed me back into my seat and left with Paul's papers still in his hand, swearing abuse at me.

At Potsdam station, the two burly Gestapo officers came to collect their prisoner and frog-marched him off the train. We had a brief farewell. Paul was brave, "Don't worry, Thomas. I'll make my way back to Berlin. Mother and Father will be pleased to see me back home."

But they never did. I know now that the next train he boarded was one of those without any seats at all. And it was not bound for Berlin.

As we continued on our way, I buried my head in my hands. Little David, sitting beside me, put his arm around me, "Are you alright, Thomas?" he asked, anxiously.

"I'm supposed to be looking after you, not the other way round."

"Do you promise me you will?"

"Of course I will," I reassured him, "We're blood brothers now."

We ate our sandwiches together and I watched the sun set as dusk made way for nightfall. Then David curled up with his head upon my shoulder and soon his steady breathing caused me to forget my anguish for the moment and close my eyes.

CHAPTER 4

We were woken up by the other boys shouting joyfully that we had crossed the border into Belgium. Here some of the 'Kinder' disembarked. Others were to leave the train in Holland. The escort was busy segregating those for their appropriate exit station. By the time we reached the Hook of Holland, the 'Kinder' carriages were half empty.

Leaving the smelly train was the only happy moment of that fateful day. My thoughts were constantly with my brother. I wondered how he was coping.

I was reminded of my new responsibility when David sought my hand to ensure we did not lose one another in the crowd. It seemed I had lost an older brother and gained a younger one.

After a long walk, we came to the dockyard. As we climbed the gangway into the passenger liner that was taking us on the next leg of our journey to England, we felt the fresh sea breeze in our faces. It was a wonderful feeling to look around and see no sign of Nazis.

Harwich was eight hours away. We were to sail through the night. After the excitement of watching the boat cast off, we stood by the rails to see the lights of Holland gradually fade as we headed for the open sea. Then I suggested we find a quiet alcove to stretch our legs and find some rest.

Our first impression of England was of torrential rain. At Harwich, the heavens opened and I saw rain as I had seldom seen it before. It was a contingency for which my mother had packed nothing.

Along with the other 'Kinder', we made our way through the downpour to a large hall where we assembled, tired and bedraggled, for processing. We found kind, maternal women waiting to look after us. They wore green uniforms with matching berets, offered us tea in large mugs and an English delicacy they called 'sausage rolls.'

Some of our party had pre-arranged sponsors waiting for them. I thought that they were the lucky ones, shipped off to London, ready for a new life. The rest of us were interviewed each in turn for particulars of our interests and backgrounds. My 'green' lady was sympathetic to my request that David and I should stay together.

David and I were amongst thirty-four 'Kinder' bound for Dovercourt, a summer camp, from where we hoped to be 'found' by a friendly family. I woke David to tell him the good news. He managed a drowsy smile,

"Thank you, Thomas. I want to stay with you forever."

Dovercourt was no holiday camp. Overcrowded dormitories, inedible food, and many sad, uprooted children who had been waiting for weeks in vain to be found homes. But everyone was kind and eager to help; there were no Nazis and that was excellent compensation for the discomfort.

Now that I had an address, my first task was to write two letters. The first was to my parents letting them know that I was safe and well. I told them of Paul's arrest in Potsdam and wrote: *'I am sure he is back home now and none the worse for his journey.'* Next, I wrote to my beloved Gisela, who had forever been in my thoughts. I explained the circumstances of my unexpected departure and begged her to reply to my letter at once.

All I remember of Dovercourt is boredom and waiting. Waiting to be found a home, waiting for replies to my letters.

Fourteen days into my stay, a solitary letter arrived: five pages of closely written lines from my parents.

They were shocked to hear about Paul, from whom they had heard not a word. The oppression had got worse; it was no longer safe to go out in the streets. Yet, father was going to risk a trip to Potsdam to try and find out where Paul was and get him home. They promised to write every other day. And so they did. Receiving their letters was the highlight of my life, but there was still no response from Gisela. I wrote again, emptied my heart to her, with expression of my deep, everlasting love. After that, all I could do was to wait, hope and pray.

The next letter from my parents was alarming. Father had got back safely from Potsdam, but with no news of Paul. The Police either didn't know or wouldn't tell.

I was still waiting for something to happen after six long boring weeks, when I was summoned to the office. There was a 'home' going for a 'strong, healthy boy' to work on a farm. It sounded a great opportunity; I loved animals and fresh air. I accepted at once, but had to ask whether my ten-year old 'brother' could come as well. David and I spent two days in suspense. More waiting. When the answer came, David could hardly contain his happiness. He jumped up down and hugged me, the trauma of leaving his family briefly forgotten. I was his 'father figure' and gave him security in exile. It made me feel very mature.

We were met at Liverpool Street Station by a tall, grey-haired man, who introduced himself as 'Mack'. We all piled into a dilapidated Land Rover, drove through London and after one hour, arrived at a small town called Rickmansworth. From there, we took the road to Chorleywood. A sharp right turn into Rasehill Farm led us to the place that was to be home for we knew not how long.

There to welcome us was Mack's wife, Maureen, a smiling woman with babe in arms. I understood English well enough to follow that the baby, christened Jean, had been born only four weeks ago. Maureen spoke a little German and, with a mixture of languages, we got on very well. We learnt that the farm was the hobby of a wealthy industrialist, who employed Mack to produce milk, butter and poultry in sufficient quantity to feed the two families and divide between them any profits that might be over.

The smallholding comprised fifteen acres, on which they kept some two thousand poultry, mostly chickens, but also turkeys, ducks and geese. There were six cows and eight pigs. Mack was running the farm single-handed, and I was to be trained as his assistant. My wages were to be five pounds per week with free lodging and produce. David was offered two pounds as a starting point, to be increased if he proved useful. In the event, he was indefatigable. He took to all his tasks as the proverbial 'duck to water'.

Mack taught us all he knew. Within seven days we were milking the cows – a strange experience. Mack insisted on total cleanliness and stood over us while we scrubbed our hands in disinfectant before letting us loose on the udders. The cows all had names and must have been bilingual as we addressed them in German. I developed an affinity with them and chatted to them whilst milking. I loved their smell and enjoyed leading them to pasture after they had produced gallons of creamy milk. We learnt how to pasteurise the milk and segregate the cream for butter and cheese. After a month, we had acquired such expertise, that we might have been doing it all our lives.

I was less enthusiastic about our chickens, which David made his speciality. He loved mixing their feed and have them besiege the loaded wheelbarrow as he drove it into the pen. He had a special relationship with them and some became so tame that they would feed from his hand. We had to get used to the dirty side of keeping animals and spent many hours each day cleaning the yard and sheds.

Another duty was added to the many that we performed. Mack and Maureen had not been out together since the birth of their daughter. It was a reflection of their trust in us, that they asked us one Saturday if we would baby-sit for them. We must have done it well for they asked us to do the same the following Saturday and the one after. It became a routine. They were such a lovely couple, that I was happy to be of service to them.

With the traditional night-out spoken for, we used Friday for our relaxation instead.

Flush with the week's wages, we took one of the strange double-decker buses and enjoyed the fifteen minutes ride on the top floor to Watford, where we found a choice of six cinemas, as well as dance halls and cafes. Inevitably, we had some minor disagreements as to which films to see, there being five years between us, but we were usually pleased with the final choice. We both loved 'Fantasia' so much that we each invested a further nine pence for a second viewing.

It was as well that I had no interest in dance halls. I was saving myself for Gisela and wanted no other girl. She had not responded to my letters and I wondered whether her parents might have intercepted them. Neither had I heard from my parents since the declaration of war, and I assumed that communications had been cut. I tried to contact them through an intermediary address in neutral Switzerland, but without success.

I watched the progress of the war with alarm. I listened to the speeches of Winston Churchill on the radio. I was longing for news of a significant Nazi setback, but there was none in the early years of the war. The mighty Nazi war machine seemed unstoppable. I watched the newsreels to see the British troops pull out of France and be rescued at Dunkirk. There was much talk of a German invasion as their next aggressive move. Then what would become of us?

The Battle of Britain began with a massive air bombardment. We were close enough to London to see armadas of German bombers besiege the city. We heard the bombs explode and saw clouds of smoke mushroom in the sky. I shuddered when the planes flew low enough to show their black crosses and swastikas. On one occasion, I even saw the bombs tumbling downwards. Suddenly the Nazis were violating the seclusion that we had found in rural England. I feared that worse might follow.

One afternoon in September, I was helping David feed the chickens, when three German Junkers flew quite low overhead. Instinctively, I grabbed David and threw him into a nearby ditch. From our protected position, we watched spellbound as a solitary Spitfire dived out of the sun with guns blazing. And a bomber was hit! With smoke pouring from its engine, it spiralled earthwards. We saw two parachutes open as the crew baled out. The Spitfire was going for another 'kill' as they all disappeared from sight.

David and I cheered at the destruction of an enemy plane. We heard that it hit a field in Amersham about six miles away, and that the crew were arrested not far from the wreckage.

I studied the papers every day to see how many planes were shot down. I said to Mack, "One hundred and sixty-seven down today – a record. Soon they will stop coming."

And one week later they did.

Mack said, "I think we've won the Battle of Britain."

I loved Churchill's speech, 'Never has so much been owed by so many to so few.' I felt proud of my adopted country.

But, even though the bombing had stopped, the news was not good. The Nazis were consolidating their grip on Europe, whilst converging the full might of their armies into Northern Africa.

On 4th November 1942 at El Alemein, the German armies were thrown into retreat with heavy casualties. Mr. Churchill had the church bells rung in celebration. People were cheering in the streets. Strangers were congratulating each other. It was the first decisive battle the Allies had won and they didn't lose another.

Three months later, I was snatched from the tranquillity of my happy farming days to serve in His Majesty's Army. My adopted country needed me. I was eighteen, and it was time for me to do my bit for King and Country. I was not unhappy at the chance of hitting back. Besides, I had an inkling it might take me closer to Gisela.

CHAPTER 5

"Jerry's gonna laugh in yer face if yer do it like that," the Sergeant screamed at me. "He'll skin yer alive if that's the best yer can do,"

When it came to fixing bayonet and howling obscenities whilst repeatedly stabbing a straw dummy, I was frankly unconvincing. My rifle drill was below average. Bloody awful, the Sergeant called it – "There's a bloody war on. God 'elp us with you out there."

But shooting the thing was even worse. I tended to miss the target more often than not in anticipation of the recoil that had already turned my shoulder black and blue.

The basic training as an infantryman in the Essex Regiment was gruelling. Unheated barracks at Colchester in the depth of a cold winter did little to inspire enthusiasm for army drill. I was finding it difficult to deal effectively with the two items that ruled my life: my rifle and boots. Wearing the boots was bad enough, but shining them so as not to incur the Sergeant's wrath was an insurmountable challenge.

I was the butt of the platoon jokes. But, inept as I was with my kit, I was tall and strong and able to hold my own in tests of physical endurance. I surprised my mates by winning the five-mile run that started our day every morning at six am. I made sure that the Sergeant knew about it too.

I would have mastered the rifle in the end, but fate intervened. I was summoned to the office of our adjutant, Major Gregson. It had come to his notice that I was bilingual. There were better uses for a fluent German-speaker than as a foot soldier. A transfer would rob the regiment of its most untalented soldier, and help the War Effort in other areas.

A week later, I was seconded to the Intelligence Corps, based at Army HQ Catterick. Here, I joined a motley group of men in uniform, whose only common denominator was their command of the German language. We were to be trained for missions as yet unspecified.

Captain Vic Spielmann, himself a German refugee, was in charge of us. His approach to our duties was refreshingly light-hearted, but he let us know that this was no 'cushy skive.' We could be called upon to work in any area where our knowledge of the enemy's language could be put to best use. It might be as dangerous as spying in occupied Europe or as mundane as interviewing POWs. Upon completion of our training, details of which were sparse, we were to be given promotion to the rank of Second Lieutenant, perhaps beyond if we showed promise.

As I was the youngest in the group, Captain Spielmann took a personal interest in my development. He chose me to accompany him to Plymouth, where the surviving crew of the German submarine, U49, was in captivity. Their vessel had been rammed by a Destroyer after depth charges had forced it to the surface. Only the seventeen men who were able to dive into the ocean were taken prisoner; the rest perished.

I learnt a lot from Vic's technique. He was to interview each in turn. Before the first one was marched in, he said to me, "We both hate their guts. Of course we do. But never show your animosity. You have to come over as their friend. Let them be arrogant and surly, if they wish. Most will be. But it's our job to extract maximum information from them and this is best done by appearing to be on their side, with the help of our common language."

I was to be reminded of these words many times as my new career unfolded.

Most of the seamen we were to interview were hard-bitten Nazis, who had sworn allegiance to their Führer. Previous interrogation by an English officer had revealed no more than name, rank and number. Vic would expect to extract more.

The first of the survivors was marched in, an armed escort either side of him. He wore a heavily stained white-turned-grey, sweater with polo neck, no jacket and seamen's trousers. His face had not seen a razor for many months and his style-less ginger hair hung limp about his ears and forehead. He had a determined, yet depressed, look about him now that he had been divested of his power.

The Captain rose as he entered, offered him a chair and a hand-shake, which he declined. On the defensive, the prisoner clicked his heels and raised his arm in the traditional salute. "Heil Hitler!"

The Captain responded to the salute in clear dialect-free German. "Oh, I don't think we need to be formal in here. Your name is…..?"

At being addressed in his mother tongue, the prisoner visibly relaxed, "Hans Dieter."

The Captain shuffled seventeen sheets of paper until he came to the one that bore the name of the man in front of him. All it gave was name, rank and number. The space headed 'comments' was blank, indicating that the previous interview had yielded nothing more.

Vic was about to illustrate how the friendly approach would show results, although his subject looked anything but friendly. "Are they looking after you alright, Hans?"

"Yes."

"Nice English food," he pulled a grimace at the thought of it. "Is it enough for you?"

"No. I am always hungry."

"Anything I can do for you?"

"Yes. Send me home." The prisoner actually broke into a smile.

Vic had scored a point. He carried on the joke. "When would you like to leave?"

"Today…..tomorrow….soon."

Smiling, Vic said, "I'll see what I can do for you. I'm sure it won't be long. Meanwhile, you're safe now and your family will be advised by the Red Cross. Should your parents be contacted, or do you have your own family?"

"I have a wife and a baby daughter."

"How old is she?"

"She's nearly four months now."

Vic didn't look up from writing his notes as he asked the first leading question, "You've never seen her then? What a shame." Vic wrote 'at sea at least four months'. "How long were you with the U47?"

"It is the only ship I have served on."

"So you must know your way around it quite well. What was your job?"

The prisoner looked at his grease-stained hands before he replied, "In the machine room."

"Did you have any excitement on this tour?"

"Yes."

"You sank some ships? How many?"

"I can't remember." He didn't want to incriminate himself.

"Well was it ten, fifteen, twenty?"

"Nothing like that." Anxious to minimise the scale of the submarine's aggression.

"Shall we settle for maybe eight?"

"More like six."

"Do you remember the names of any of the ships you sank?"

"I can't remember all. I think one was called 'Hastings'."

Vic referred to a file. He noted that a cargo ship called SS Hastings, thirty five thousand tons, had been torpedoed in mid-Atlantic on the night of 24th January 1942. All crew perished at sea.

"Any others?"

"I can't remember."

"If you have been patrolling for six months, you must have been running short of torpedoes?"

"We were on our way home when the attack took place."

"And where is home?" Vic asked, conversationally.

"I'm not allowed to answer that question. Geneva Convention."

"Yes, of course. I don't know why I bothered to ask. We all know that the U47 was launched at Bremen in July '41, and had its own berth there, waiting for its return. We even know the route it took by the Scapa Flow heading for the Atlantic."

The cut and thrust of the interrogation continued for another twenty minutes, by which time foolscap sheets of notes had been completed. Vic felt he had extracted as much information as he was going to get from the first session and terminated the interview.

He turned to me, "How d'you think that worked?"

"I was impressed with your technique."

"Good," he said, "I'll take two more of the bastards today and then it's your turn."

Thus started my contribution to the War Effort that was to absorb my interests for the next three years.

CHAPTER 6

I was moved around from one camp to another, plying my newly found trade with reasonable results. At first it was fascinating to confront the enemy on a one-to-one basis, but most interrogations followed a familiar pattern, which made the routine monotonous. Vic's friendly approach often provoked defiance and arrogance, and it was not easy to be friendly towards prisoners who showed no sense of guilt for the carnage the regime had created. Indeed, they often went on the offensive and responded with odious Nazi ideology before being told to 'shut up.' I derived some satisfaction from having the upper hand and no longer being the victim of their racial hatred.

But one man struck an open nerve. He had spent a year working at Belsen and told me stories of what he had seen that made me vomit. It was his opinion that no Jew would survive the concentration camps. "The system is geared to their total extermination," he said without emotion. It made me feel ill. I terminated the interview at once.

There was no means of communication with my family. By March '43, the Red Cross was still unable to issue lists of detainees and where they might be, if indeed they were still alive. There had been alarming rumours of massacres. Heart-rending pictures and letters had been smuggled out of the camps. They reached the West by courtesy of neutral states and were studied by shocked relatives. Sometimes, the fate of their loved ones was never established and they lived only to wait, fearing the worst, but still hoping.

With the Russian victory at Stalingrad, the Germans in full retreat and thousands of American GI's assembled in Britain, the final outcome of the war was no longer in doubt. The invasion of France was clearly in preparation, and I was longing for our forces to reach the camps and finally reveal their dreadful secrets.

There was jubilation when the invasion armada finally set off for France on June 6th '44. Even though decisive battles lay ahead at which there would be many casualties, Churchill's 'beginning of the end' was now in sight. Once the bridgeheads in France had been established, there would be much work to be done by my group. Interviewing POWs whilst the heat of battle was within earshot, assumed far greater importance.

Vic, two others and I were flown to France on 24th June, and were quickly deployed interviewing prisoners, whose capture might have happened within the hour. We were operating five miles behind the front line in conjunction with Army Officers assessing enemy positions and trying to establish their strength. The information obtained could affect the outcome of current battles, even the war itself.

We were confronted with battle-weary soldiers of all ranks. Some were surly and arrogant, others dejected and gloomy but nonetheless relieved that their war was over.

The newsreels and papers were full of horror stories and gruesome pictures as the world was informed of six million Jewish dead.

I had to wait until June 20th 1945 before I received confirmation of the news I was dreading to hear. The last known record of my family had shown that they were 'shipped' to Buchenwald concentration camp in November '39. My father was treating inmate patients until late '43, at which point the trail stopped abruptly. My brother is known to have survived two years at Dachau before he died. Causes unknown.

Although I was expecting the news, I was shocked and stunned when confirmation finally arrived. I sat on my bed, my head in my hands and wept.

CHAPTER 7

With the end of the war, our work became even more demanding. Every male German was our prisoner and a good few females were suspected of war crimes too. We concentrated on those in uniform, conducting a process that became known as 'de-Nazification.' They all swore innocence and it became our job to isolate the 'criminals' for trial.

Now that I knew the fate of my family, I had a burning hatred of all German personnel. My questioning of them was no longer unbiased. They were all guilty of genocide. I could no longer tolerate a conversation with them on whatever terms. I longed to be released from my post.

It came to my notice that a Forces Radio Station was setting up in Cologne. They were holding auditions for announcers, news-readers and presenters. I wanted to stay in Germany for a while. And so I applied.

They told me I had a good voice, read well and had the cosmopolitan approach to music that they sought.

Within four weeks I was on air. At first, I was painfully nervous. When the red lights flashed 'go', I feared that the listeners would hear my pounding heart. But, in time, I overcame my nerves. I enjoyed the work and the minor degree of fame that came with it.

I felt no inclination to terminate my career in the Forces now that I had found my niche. Besides, I had an ulterior motive for wanting to prolong my stay in Cologne. I had appointed a German solicitor to press a heavy claim against the German state. The indictment, covering loss of life and limb, property, business and education, ran to eight pages. To its credit, the new Government was negotiating restitution settlements and I felt that my claims could be more easily enforced whilst I was 'local.' At the same time, I felt the urgent need to revisit Berlin. I needed to return to the city in which

I had spent my early youth, to see for myself what had become of my family home. Berlin, now under Russian control, was not easily accessible but now my solicitors insisted that I make the trip, since the state of the family property was a vital ingredient of my claim.

I walked the streets of Berlin amidst the ruins. I was used to seeing towns that had suffered heavy aerial bombardment, but devastation on this scale was new to me. Whole streets had been obliterated. Few buildings had escaped damage. Exterior walls were still standing in some cases with hollow interiors.

Many of the landmarks I had known so well had disappeared. I looked for the buildings and street corners where I had used to dodge the Gestapo. Most were beyond recognition. The swastikas were now replaced by Hammer & Sickle insignia. Armies of occupation were to be seen everywhere. The shops that were still standing mostly had shutters pulled down. A few grocery shops were open with little produce to offer their starving customers. I needed to make detours where some streets were inaccessible.

I found my way, with difficulty to Tauntzien Strasse, and stood outside the building that had used to be home. Miraculously, the front wall was still standing. Even the door through which I had passed so often was there, clinging to its frame by the last two hinges. The tarnished gold plaque still attached to the door had used to have my father's name embossed upon it. I noted in my diary the names of the most recent occupants: 'Doktor Heinz Bochmann and Doktor Gerda Bochmann.' No doubt a medical couple who had commandeered my father's practice and premises. I wondered whether they had still been working there when the building was destroyed.

I pulled the door open and stepped inside. The dust lay thick on the ground. The air was musty and heavy with pollution. I walked up the five steps to where the lift had once been. It was no more. The stairway to the upper floors, too, had gone. The surrounding walls were jagged; no more than six feet tall at their highest point. The filthy remains of what had been a luxurious red carpet were still visible, now ravaged by the elements.

I sat on the steps amongst the rubble that had been my home and looked up at the sky. The memories crowded in on me. I closed my eyes and felt their presence. I felt my father's reassuring hand on my shoulder, my mother's light kiss upon my brow, heard them speak once more, watched them move. I heard my brother's care-free laughter. For a brief moment we were all united.

And then I stared into the abyss. For what fear, what anguish, what unimaginable horrors had they faced? My dearest mother and father. At the end, had they even been allowed to stay together? I stayed in that derelict hallway for maybe ten minutes more, immersed in my dark thoughts. There was nothing to be gained by staying longer.

I got to my feet, began to take photographs of the building for the lawyers as though it was simply a job of work. I knew I would never return.

I crossed the city and after half an hour's walk, I reached my destination. The house I sought was standing and inhabited. Its neighbour had been less fortunate. I smoothed my hair. The Russians had advised that I wear civilian clothes. I was wearing a borrowed, fawn suit. I shook the dust from its folds straightened my tie and opened the gate that led through the small garden to the front door. It was a neat house in some need of repair, owned by a family of modest means. There was an air of dilapidation. Two of the front windows were cracked and the garden was overgrown and untended.

I rang the doorbell.

I heard a voice from within that I recognised at once, "I'll get it."

The door was opened by a woman holding a baby in her arms. Gisela. There was a stunned silence as we looked at one another. She looked worn out, emaciated and aged beyond her years. Her greasy blond hair showed dark roots. She was still attractive in a down-and-out type of way, but I was shocked to see the lines etched around her eyes.

She swallowed hard, "Thomas, I can't believe it after all this time."

I kissed her on the cheek, "Hallo, Gisela. How are you?"

She said, "You look so handsome now. You always were, but now you look handsome, grown up."

The baby began to cry. She placed it on her shoulder and, turning back into the house, called out, "Mutti, I have a visitor.

Could you take Wolfgang?"

Her mother came out, took the little one and gave me a smile.

With hands free, Gisela patted her hair in a vain attempt to improve its appearance, "You should have phoned me first," she said, "I look terrible, I know I do." She smiled at me and as she did so, I saw the face as I had remembered it all those years ago. The beautiful teeth, the dimples, the coy charm: poignant reminders of my first love affair.

"I wrote you so many letters," I said, "and you didn't reply, so, as I was in Berlin, I thought I'd come and see for myself what's happened to you."

"It was difficult to write to you, with my parents and the war..."

She changed the subject, not wanting to get into a racial conflict. I knew that her family were Nazis and anti-semitic.

"Are you married?"

I shook my head.

"Engaged?"

I shook my head again.

"I'm sure you have a lot of girlfriends." She smiled at the thought. I resisted the urge to tell her that I had been saving myself for her. I told her my story first and how unhappy I was to have left so quickly without saying goodbye.

"That was awful," she said," I waited for two hours. I cried all week when you didn't come to school. I couldn't understand why you had left me."

"I didn't want to. I thought of nothing but you for months after."

"Months only?" she asked, with a sly smile.

With every minute I spent in her company, the passion of years ago was re-awakened.

We were still on the doorstep. "Aren't you going to invite me in?" I asked.

She looked embarrassed, "I will tell you Thomas, it is very difficult with my mother. She will not allow any boyfriends in the house."

I noticed that she had focused on the Star of David hanging around my neck. It was a glance that spoke volumes. I understood.

We walked to the corner, sat on the low wall of the bombed house where builders were at work. I listened intently as she told me how

29

tragedy had touched her life in equal measure to my own. Her father and brother had both been killed in the Russian campaign. She had found brief happiness in 1944, when she had married Axel. He died in an air raid and did not live to see the birth of his son, Wolfgang. Her mother had been pleased to have daughter and grandson move in with her but, without their men-folk, the women found the financial pressures intolerable. Gisela was obliged to find employment. Not easy in post-war Berlin. She looked after Wolfgang by day and went to work at night. She was reluctant to say exactly what she did, but inadvertent mention of 'the club', led me to my own conclusion. The nightclub industry was the first to flourish in Berlin and the girls earned big money entertaining the troops.

"I seldom get home until the early hours. I only snatch a few hours sleep before the baby wakes."

"You're looking tired. Is it not too much for you, the work and the baby?"

"What can I do?" she replied, and with a twinkle in her eye, "Marry me Thomas. Take us away to a beautiful sunny island: just the three of us. Wouldn't that be wonderful?" She burst out laughing at the prospect as though she had cracked the funniest joke.

Perhaps it was the expression on my face that made her laugh so. It was the first proposal of marriage I had ever received, even if spoken in jest. A few years earlier, I would have taken her, come what may. Now everything had changed.

"Do you propose to every man who turns up on your doorstep, Gisela?" I teased her.

"You are not every man, Thomas. A girl does not forget her first love." She smiled innocently, "You remember our little 'hideaway' in the woods?"

"Of course. How could I forget?"

"Shall we meet there just for old times' sake?"

It was the last thing I expected, but talking to Gisela stimulated my appetite for her, "That would be very romantic," I said.

"Give me an hour to feed Wolfgang, make myself look pretty for you and I'll meet you there."

I arrived first and cleared the entrance of its undergrowth. Nature has no respect for the needs of lovers. Once inside, the space was unchanged. Even more private, with the surrounding bushes thickened over the passing years.

When Gisela arrived, she looked glamorous. Hair styled, face made up, a décolleté blouse. I kissed her on the cheek, breathed in her perfume, muttered in her ear, "Now you look like the Gisela I remember."

In response, she put her arms around me and kissed me on the lips. She closed her eyes and did so with emotion, "It's so lovely to be with you again," she said. "I can hardly believe it."

She kissed me again. It was the most erotic experience of my life.

She had brought a rug with her. I remember it clearly – a large red and blue check with tassels along the edge. She spread it over the ground. We lay together on it that warm July afternoon in 1945. The war and conflict seemed far away. It was wonderful to feel her body so close to mine again. I was intoxicated by the fragrance of her skin. She showed considerable experience in the art of love-making. I was shy and allowed her to take control.

Afterwards, we lay on the rug, relaxing and talking of old school friends and what had become of them. Eventually, we made love again. She introduced me to variations I didn't know existed.

I would have liked to linger awhile but she looked at her watch and said, "Oh my God. How time flies. I must get back."

"It's been wonderful," I said, "Truly wonderful."

"For me too." There was hesitation before she continued, "Now that we are together again, Thomas, I have to ask you for a great favour."

"If I can, of course I will."

She was putting on her blouse as she looked at me with plaintive eyes,

"I have a big financial problem. If I cannot meet some debts on Monday, I will be arrested. They will throw us out of the house. Just imagine poor Wolfgang. Could you possibly lend me a little money? I should be able to repay you quite quickly."

I looked in my wallet and counted the notes. There was a total of four hundred and fifty deutschmarks. More than I usually carried with me in case I was obliged to stay overnight. I counted out the notes into the palm of her hand.

"Oh Thomas," she said, staring up at me with adoration, "that is

31

so kind of you. It will help me no end. Every time I listen to you on the radio, it will remind me to repay you. It won't be long, I promise."

She may have listened, but I had no evidence that she was reminded. If she kept a record of her earnings, I am sure she would have entered the amount of four hundred deutschmarks against 'Services rendered' and not '*Loan for repayment*'.

Sadly, I never saw her again.

CHAPTER 8

When I got back to Cologne, there was an urgent call from Captain Spielmann.

"The answer's 'no', Vic," I said, " I'm not coming back."

"Hear me out, Tom, this is something quite different. Some of the bastards go on trial in November – Göring, Keitel, Speer – all the big nobs and the people that ran the camps. I'm providing the interpreters. I need you as part of my team."

"Impossible," I said, "Broadcasting's my career now." I had begun reading the news and was scheduled to start a series of my own.

"I guess this job will only take four weeks. You could easily get short term release."

"I don't want to get short term release. I'm very happy here, thank you very much."

He was silent. I sensed waves of reproach from my former mentor.

"For God's sake, Vic, you don't need me there." I reasoned, "You've plenty of translators who could do the job."

"Not as good as you. I need people I can trust. This trial will be history in the making. Your chance to see the bastards strung up. After what they did to your family... " Vic was not averse to a hitting below the belt, "Come on, Thomas, what's four weeks?"

"Who's to say it will just take four weeks? They've got lawyers, haven't they? They'll stretch it out as long as they can..."

"Four weeks. I promise you," he lied, "They're all guilty as hell. How could it take any longer?"

CHAPTER 9

Seeing the ruins of Nüremberg for the first time, from the back seat of an army jeep, I found it hard to remember that this had once been a prosperous city. Most of the houses had been reduced to rubble. Some had walls still standing. Those that had not been hit were scarred by the bombs and only just habitable.

"Hey, Chuck, let's stop, can we?" Nathan called out to the driver. "Let Tom see where he's going to be working."

Captain Nathan Grunfeld – a fellow translator who had been given the task of settling me in. Only a little chap, but a lot to say for himself. We had already established that we shared the same town of birth and had even attended the same school. He was a few years older than me, which is why our paths hadn't crossed before. The army driver pulled up. We jumped down from the jeep and shook the dust from our uniforms.

We stared up at the Palace of Justice. It was an imposing sight. Miraculously, almost as though by some higher design, the building was about the only thing that was relatively undamaged. With one thousand or more prison cells within its walls, it had become first choice of location for the trial. The Russians had argued the point, as they had argued over every issue, that the trial should be staged in Berlin, which, though theoretically divided between the four conquering nations, was virtually under their control. Nüremberg was in the American zone, where the U.S. had full jurisdiction and, with support from England and France, they were able to prevail. The theory was that holding the trial here in this former Nazi stronghold, scene of so many torch lit mass rallies, would add to the demoralisation of the German people.

We went inside. There was a lot of building work going on. Nathan explained, "The courtroom's being virtually rebuilt. They're making it double the size to allow for the twenty-two prisoners, their defending council, prosecution, judges and a visitors' gallery".

"You mean the courtroom isn't even finished yet?" I exclaimed.

It seemed that work would finish only hours before the trial was to open. The smell of fresh paint and the glare of new lighting and spotlights were very apparent.

We went down to the cells that were awaiting their occupants. No one had bothered to give them attention. They were dirty and smelly. The walls were covered in mildew, excreta and graffiti. They had probably not been cleaned since they were built several centuries before, having housed since then, the local convicts for many decades.

On arrival, the imprisoned Nazis were to be allocated cleaning materials, buckets of water; paint and brushes, so that they could choose to live in squalor or to make an attempt to remove the stale musty smell of stench, sweat and hardship left by previous occupants.

They were fortunate to be still alive. The Russians had wanted to hang the whole gang summarily, without trial. And who could blame a country whose population had been so ravaged by the German invaders, for seeking revenge? But the western powers wanted the world to witness a fair trial, so that the crimes of the murderous Nazi regime could be documented and made public. For the world, too, wanted revenge.

Sadly, the principal players of the Third Reich could not be present. Adolf Hitler had shot himself, hours before the Russians could take him in his underground bunker. Arch criminal Himmler, had taken poison after he was taken prisoner, and Goebbels, infamous mouthpiece of the party, had offered cyanide to his wife and six small children, before shooting himself.

I was installed with Nathan in the Officer's quarters of the former Nazi Adelberg Barracks. The accommodation was sparse but adequate: a room to myself with a washbasin and shower separated by a plastic curtain. The bed was hard and narrow and, as I settled down for my first night's sleep, I wondered who the previous occupant had been.

It was a ten-minute bus ride to the Palace of Justice. We hadn't been on the bus for five minutes of bland small talk, when Nathan burst into his 'Hitler routine.' Quoting from a well-publicised Führer speech in German, he had the intonation and expressions down to a fine art. The laughter from those sitting around us encouraged him. He stood up to embrace his wider audience. He brushed his hair forward, placed a finger over his upper lip, for moustache, and performed to the great amusement of all on board.

He was a joker from the start of our acquaintance and it wasn't until I knew him better that I was to appreciate the deeper qualities of the man. Considering the nature of our posting and the harrowing evidence we were to hear, it was a pleasantly light-hearted start to the long haul that lay ahead. Just how long the haul might be, would soon be apparent by our total inactivity for the first month, while procedural wrangles were debated in court.

"So much for my one month posting," I complained to Vic, "I'll be lucky if it's over in one year, the speed we're moving."

He leaned back, unperturbed, "I'm sorry, dear boy, but time is of little significance when a page of history is being written. Imagine; you'll be able to tell your children that you played a part in the biggest trial the world has ever seen. I tell you, this is a fitting end to your military career that one day you'll be proud of."

"Some consolation," I said to Nathan, as I listened, enviously, to my colleagues on the BFN radio station.

We spent many hours in the canteen at the courtroom just waiting in total inactivity. When there is nothing to do but talk and drink tea, it is surprising how relationships can develop. I had formed a 'blood brother' friendship with Nathan Grunfeld. We spent days and nights in each other's company. It was never boring; he was a natural raconteur. His stories were full of humour and told with great panache.

On a Sunday morning, when we had nothing better to do than sit and talk, he made a remarkable statement. Filling his pipe, he sat back, and with a rhetorical flourish said, "You know, my life was saved by Great Art and I really mean Great Art."

"Interesting," I replied, "how come?"

There was a pause in the conversation while he flattened the tobacco and lit the pipe. He sucked away and moments later, clouds of smoke polluted the air. Even then he did not reply immediately, allowing the smoke to curl about his nose, while he recalled the events that saved his life. The more he told me, the more I wanted to hear. Three hours, six cups of coffee and four pipes later I said to him, "What an amazing story. You should write a book. Compulsive reading I dare say."

"Writing's not for me. I haven't the patience."

I looked at my watch, whilst he filled his pipe once again. We had no plans for the rest of the day. I said casually, "Suppose I were to write your story?"

"That's fine," was his repartee, "as long as we share the royalties."

I doubted if it would ever get that far, but agreed readily.

"It's a done deal, partner," he said in his pseudo American voice, "I do the talking, you do the writing." He added with a smile, "But do me a favour, make me a bit taller and a helluva lot more attractive."

I didn't realize at the time the scale of the task that I was under-taking with very little prior consideration. It was the inactivity that drove me to it. I said, "You'll have to search your memory for every minute detail you can remember. He said with a chuckle, "There are two things in life I enjoy. One is screwing; the other is talking. About myself if possible."

I went to the office to borrow a clipboard and as many sheets of foolscap as they would release. When I returned and settled in my chair opposite him, I said, "I think this is quite an exciting moment."

For reply, he blew smoke into the air.

"Now, where should we start….."

NATHAN'S STORY
CHAPTER 10

Berlin 1932! The city was a hotbed of culture: music, art, opera, and theatre. Performances of the highest quality by the world's leading artists. Music-lovers were spoilt for choice – Otto Klemperer's 'Ring', Bruno Walter's Beethoven cycle with Artur Schnabel playing the piano concerti and Casals the cello Sonatas. There was Toscanini, as a frequent guest conductor with the Berlin Philharmonic and appearances by a young genius of eight years old, Yehudi Menuhin who played the most complex violin repertoire while still a little lad in a sailor suit.

There was a wide selection of contemporary and modern plays presented at the theatres, poetry and prose readings from Heinrich Heine to Thomas Mann. Art exhibitions: Picasso, Renoir, Matisse.

On the lighter side there was Kurt Weill's Threepenny opera and Marlene Dietrich appearing in provocative cabaret. And even lighter, there was no reason why a single gentleman might not enjoy his favoured entertainment followed by a night of passion. Girls of outstanding beauty, some with intellect as well, could be seen on every street corner and could be engaged in conversation or whatever, at most Kaffeehaüser, bars or night-clubs. The girls knew what was wanted of them and the young enthusiast was quick to take advantage.

Here was German decadence and culture at its height. The participants of this colourful life were so absorbed in their activities that they could be excused for barely noticing Hitler, his oncoming Nazi party and its virulent anti-semitism.

Arthur Grunfeld sat in the Music room tuning his cello. It was a spacious room with white walls and ceiling, from which there hung a modest chandelier. Beside him stood a shining black Bechstein piano, and opposite, two settees surrounded by eight small upright gold chairs. Along the far wall was a music library crammed with most great works in the chamber music repertoire. A perfect setting for 'Soirées Musicales,' which often took place there.

He was awaiting the arrival of his accompanist and, satisfied that his instrument was in tune, he began to play a familiar theme and then to improvise variations. The expression on his face reflected the mood of the piece. At thirty-eight years of age, he was at the peak of his musical ability, the master of his craft.

He looked relaxed this Saturday morning away from the stress of his fashion factory. He wore a blue shirt, a floppy suede jacket and a spotted bow tie. Even for the office, he liked to wear a bow tie. It seemed to give expression to his artistic inclinations. He was a good looking man with strong lines to his face, an aquiline nose. He wore his prematurely greying hair swept back without parting. His blue eyes were penetrating and could be stern, particularly when Ilse kept him waiting. Such a moment it now was. He broke off abruptly, rose to his feet, and carefully standing his cello against the wall, went out into the hall, shouting, "Ilse, where in God's name are you?"

Dutifully, she arrived almost at once in the doorway. She was an attractive woman, of Slavic appearance with green eyes, high cheekbones, and glossy black hair. "Sorry darling, I was doing Nathan's homework with him. Ridiculous what they expect him to do at his age."

Arthur calmed down, "I've got to leave in twenty minutes. I have to see Fassmann at the office. I think we'll do *Opus 69* again, shall we?" It was the *Beethoven Sonata No.3* that they had been practising the previous day.

Ilse sat at the piano, removed the four jangly bracelets from her wrist, and sounded the 'A' chord. There was something bohemian about her appearance today. She wore a v-necked sweater in deep orange with a toning silk scarf draped around her neck.

Eight-year old Nathan came in, threw himself down on the settee, pretending to study his book, as though trying to understand the complexities of German grammar. He was a good-looking boy with curly hair and a cheeky smile, a little on the portly side. He enjoyed his food.

Arthur said, "Let's do it from start to finish." He loved this sonata more than most, not least because the cello solo introduced the main sonorous theme. He looked lovingly at Ilse, while he played it by heart. As she accompanied her husband, she looked young enough to be in her first year of Music Academy.

The performance went flawlessly. As they went into the sparkling Rondo of the last movement, Nathan took the role of conductor. Not only waving his arms in time to the music, but also singing the theme in a high-pitched treble voice until the triumphant conclusion. At this point, he took a bow, whilst his parents applauded.

These were the happier moments of life in Berlin, where the Grunfelds enjoyed the luxury of their modern house in Grunewald, an exclusive suburb of the capital. But the storm clouds of oppression and anti-semitism were gathering.

Arthur could not believe that he and his family would be subjected to the threat of violence that peppered all the speeches. He was a law-abiding citizen of the German Empire, who had taken his place, as had all good Germans, in the Kaiser's army of 1914 –18. His musical prowess had kept him out of the trenches – he had played in the regimental band - but he had still worn the uniform and been prepared to lay down his life for the Fatherland. In the event, the closest he came to seeing action was when the band entertained troops who were on leave ten kilometres behind the front line.

After the Great War, in common with some two million battle-weary soldiers returning from the front, he had experienced the inevitable sense of vacuum on demob. Arthur had filled it by playing in a tea dance café. Post war, defeated and demoralised, the German people had not yet been ready to tea dance and his engagement there was short-lived.

His brother Walter, meanwhile, had been working for a small factory that produced sweaters and scarves for the troops. When the factory's only customer, the State, ceased to operate, so did the factory. The brothers were quick to take it over and for next to nothing. Theirs was one of the first new post war companies to be registered. W. & A. Grunfeld. The product was elegant ladies' knitwear, a field they pioneered with great enthusiasm and success.

So much so that, over the years, the tiny nucleus company grew into one of the most powerful groups in Europe. The brothers were proud of their German heritage, proud to be playing their part in alleviating the agony of defeat and its humiliation after the war.

Arthur continued his cello engagements whenever possible, and was playing in the orchestra under Otto Klemperer in a performance of *Missa Solemnis*, while Ilse sang in the choir. They had been staring and smiling at each other long before they met. When they did and Arthur discovered that his beautiful choirgirl acquaintance had trained to be a concert pianist, and that she was the daughter of an eminent Jewish doctor in Berlin, marriage became inevitable.

Ilse made a wonderful job of furnishing their spacious home. It was contemporary but comfortable, extravagant but with none of the nouveau-riche trappings that a decorator of less confident taste might have felt the need to introduce.

Arthur held the purse string securely. He put his foot down if he felt expenditure exceeded the budget. If indeed he ever had a budget. Its figure was never disclosed and he would use it as an excuse if there were an idea or purchase of which he disapproved.

It happened following Ilse's shopping spree at the Templemann Art Gallery. She had fallen in love with a group of six Renoir oils of incredible colour and luminosity. *La Baigneuse* was exquisite. She could not take her eyes off it. A view of *La Seine* with people enjoying the sunshine, was even more striking. Such colour and light. The price would be an equivalent of today's four thousand pounds for all six, a lot of money in those days and Arthur would not hear of it.

"Sorry darling, far too much... the budget just can't take it. Only yesterday I added all the expenditures. Way beyond our means... just running out of money."

Ilse knew exactly how to handle him. She snuggled close and kissed him on the cheek, "Artie," She always abbreviated his name when she wanted something, "those paintings are the most beautiful I have ever seen and we just must have them. Remember how we agreed to leave the walls plain white, so that we could hang them with wonderful pictures?"

He hated to veto any suggestion his wife made, but held his

ground.

She continued, "Mr. Templemann at the gallery says they are increasing in value by the day. We can enjoy them and have a great investment at the same time."

"Darling, we've spent much more on the house than planned and we're way over budget," he repeated.

"Why don't you come down to the gallery, meet Mr. Templemann, view the paintings and see how you feel about them?" she persisted.

He mumbled some more about his budget but agreed to visit the gallery. Ilse knew what the result would be.

Arthur was stunned by the beauty of the pictures. In fact, Ilse swore afterwards that she saw his eyes moisten when he first saw them. He was clearly moved. Mr. Templemann was fussing around them, excited at the prospect of a six-picture sale. Over coffee and Streusselkuchen, the deal was done, but not before Arthur was able to negotiate a small reduction.

Outside the gallery, the Grunfelds embraced. "My darling Artie, I am so happy. You were so clever to get them a little more cheaply. Now, we are within the budget, yes?"

The pictures were delivered the next day and with an accompanying bouquet of a dozen red roses. The card was a personal note from Mr. Templemann wishing them much happiness with the pictures.

"What a sweet man," Ilse thought as she set about the joyous task of hanging them.

The Music Room was the most important room in the house. So it was here that Ilse decided to hang three of the Renoirs. *The Piano Lesson* was perfectly placed above the piano. It depicted a teacher and student. Both were girls with long willowy hair in gorgeous pastel colours. To gaze at them while playing or listening to music was to satisfy a combination of the senses at the same time. Two more of the Renoirs were hung in the Music Room and the other three, in the lounge. Ilse took considerable time hanging and lighting the pictures. She was finally satisfied that their positioning was perfect. She telephoned Arthur at his office, "Darling, you must come home this minute. I'm so excited. I have hung the Renoirs. They look fabulous. I must show you now."

"Not now, I'm in the middle of a board meeting," was his predictable reaction.

"Please Artie," she begged.

"But we're about to make a big decision."

"It can wait. You must come now," she insisted.

He could never say 'no' to his wife. He arrived home ten minutes later and was lead into the lounge first and then into the Music Room. They looked at the paintings, then at one another, then the paintings again and collapsed into each other's arms, with tears of joy welling in their eyes.

Little did they suspect that the paintings were destined to decorate the walls of Karinhall, the sumptuous country estate of Hermann Göring, Luftwaffe chief and Hitler's second in command.

CHAPTER 11

By 1933, the brothers had built a veritable empire. The turnover was multi-million and they were exporting to most countries. Additional factories had been acquired in Apolda and Vienna.

Walter was responsible for finance. They had taken on a substantial loan from 'Deutsche Bundesbank,' which required daily negotiation. Arthur's area of expertise was design. He had a good eye for colour and style that women around the world wanted to wear. Sales were robust and there was scarcely a year, in the last six, in which turnover had not doubled.

It would be wrong to say that their preoccupation with business matters made them oblivious to the impending tragedy. When Hitler became Reich Chancellor in late January of that year, Arthur felt no more comfortable than any other Jew in the country. But he resolved to stick it out, praying that the threats and aspirations which Hitler had so clearly spelled out in *Mein Kampf*, would not now be converted from rhetoric to a program for future action.

He tried to reassure himself and his family, "So, what's he going to do with us? We're Germans, just like they are… we fight for our country, we pay our taxes. There may be difficult times ahead but we've earned our position and no one's going to take that away from us."

But Ilse had other ideas. At the cinema, she had seen newsreel of Hitler's latest speech: "We will cleanse the country of this vermin… the evil Jewish parasites who alone bear the burden and responsibility for Germany's decline and defeat…"

And at the top of his voice for the final crescendo, punching the air with his clenched fist, "Germany for the Germans, a pure Aryan race free of Jewish domination." The applause had been hysterical, the swelling chorus of 'SIEG Heil, Sieg Heil' our beloved Führer', from a million massed voices, terrifying.

Afterwards, Ilse said, "We've got to get out and fast."

"And go where?"

"Anywhere. England, America, Palestine."

"And do what?"

"Does it matter as long as we get away?"

Arthur spoke placidly, in spite of the horrors of the speech, "Let's wait and see how things turn out. I'm sure his bark is worse than his bite. He could even be quite good for Germany. He'll build new roads, develop the cities, and get the nation back to work. I wouldn't be surprised if the army took back Sudetenland and I, for one, would be in favour. After all, it used to be part of Germany and should be again."

Ilse stared at him in disbelief, "I don't know why you don't just join the Party and be done with it," she said.

Arthur scowled. "Look, I hate them as much as you do. But they won't be there forever. We must accept the situation. We're Germans."

"You're wrong. We're Jewish not German, and I won't be associated with that mob. Never."

Arthur knew she was right but he wanted to close the conversation. "Look, we've built up a great business. We have a lovely home. Nathan soon goes to school. We launch our new collection next week. The whole world is waiting to see our range. I couldn't leave now, if I wanted to."

They had had this dialogue many times. Ilse was convinced their lives were in danger. She remembered her father's advice: 'History shows us that persecution of the Jews can happen in any country at any time. Always be prepared to move quickly in the face of an oppressive regime. Keep a cash reserve at home – not in the bank – at home....' he had emphasised again,... 'then you'll be able to flee at short notice. It could save your life.'

He had followed his own advice and moved to Palestine six months earlier, just as anti-semitism was reaching unprecedented levels and exploding into violence in the streets.

Her father's words had made a lasting impression on her. She intended to follow his advice and apply for an exit visa for herself, Arthur and Nathan – just in case...

CHAPTER 12

Siegfried Fassman was the one member of staff to have been retained by the Grunfelds following the take-over. His talents were a mixed blessing. Useful at the time, he had since become a nuisance as the company expanded.

Able to take a knitting machine apart and put it together again with precision, he was more technician than designer. But Siegfried had aspirations to take over the design department completely. He was hardly a suitable candidate – over sixty, half blind from a ricocheted bullet that had nearly killed him in World War One and with a volatile temperament - but the one eye he had left was on the main chance of becoming Managing Director.

He was a prima donna – constantly argued with Arthur, threw tantrums and walked out. But, to everyone's dismay, he always returned the next day. He was hardworking and ambitious, but his loyalty was compromised by his quest for power.

Siegfried was not slow to realise that when the Nazis took over, the Brothers Grunfeld might be exposed to some difficulty. He waited for the right moment. It came when another violent row erupted. He walked out again, but this time he did not return.

Instead, Siegfried went to SS headquarters in Bundnerallee, to have a conversation with his good friend, Major Hans Wachtel.

CHAPTER 13

Arthur and Walter sat in the boardroom waiting.

"What the hell does the bastard want?" puzzled Arthur.

"He's not coming for coffee and cakes. That's for sure," Walter replied.

Herr Major Hans Wachtel of the Waffen SS had announced his imminent arrival for a serious discussion and requested both owners of the company to be present.

The year was 1936. Hitler and his entourage had been in power for three years. They had wasted little time in implementing their promises. On March 7th, they had reclaimed the Rhineland without opposition. On August 1st of that year, the world had rewarded Nazi endeavours by staging the Olympiade in Berlin. Hitler had found himself in the world spotlight, playing host to fifty-three competing nations and able to use the sporting forum for his own political ends – to glorify the Nazi regime and to show the world how utterly he commanded the devotion of his people. While the eyes of the world were focused on German progress and unity, the Jews of Germany had a brief respite.

The games had been an undoubted success. Except for an unfortunate moment, when the black American sprinter, Jesse Owens, had won four Gold Medals, forcing the German favourite, Lutz Long, into second place, Hitler had turned his back and boycotted the presentation.

Once the final Olympic procession had brought the Games to a close, it was back to the program with a vengeance. The Reichstag was besieged by tens of thousands of party members, screaming their support in Post-Olympic frenzy. They had seen their Führer accepted and respected by the world's leaders and now the whole country seemed to be swept up in the euphoria.

For the Germans, it was a watershed. The time had come for

Hitler's followers to respond to his calls for action. For the Jews, there was little hope, as one hate-filled speech after another foreshadowed their impending demise.

The full force of the Nazi program was not yet in operation but Jews were being tormented, tortured and murdered in the streets. Shopkeepers had their windows smashed and daubed, 'Jude. Kauf nicht hier,' with a scrawled Star of David and a hangman's noose – and all with the tacit approval of the Police.

Brownshirts, Gauleiters, SS and Hitler Youth roamed the streets looking for prey, and heaven help any unfortunate Jew that crossed their path. If he denied his heritage, they would, often as not, strip him naked for confirmation. In some cases, they administered summary execution. And this was only the relatively innocuous beginning of the project.

The Grunfelds watched these sinister events with growing concern. With every news bulletin, Ilse became more frustrated. Arthur was not yet totally convinced...

The Herr Major arrived on the dot of 10 am.

"Heil Hitler," he raised his right arm in the customary salute. He was immaculately uniformed in black with jackboots and a black, white and red swastika around his upper arm. His political affiliations were in no doubt at all. He did not remove his cap throughout the meeting so that the full impact of the skull and crossbones upon it might be felt. He did not offer to shake hands but clicked his heels in military fashion as Walter showed him to a chair opposite.

He did not sit down. "I will come straight to the point," he said, "My orders are to requisition this building. It is required for Police purposes and you are requested to vacate the premises within seven days."

The brothers regarded him in stunned silence. Finally Arthur spoke, "Herr Major, are you aware that our work here is of national importance to the Reich? That the products made here are mostly for export and produce a considerable income to the benefit of the state? Furthermore, that we employ a hundred workers here, whose jobs would be lost."

"My superiors have taken this into account and made their decision accordingly."

Walter entered the dialogue with another vain effort, "We have many contracts to fulfil, which cannot be placed elsewhere..."

"Please understand that these are the requirements of the Ministry of the Interior. I am only their messenger."

"We would like to consult our solicitor to see whether we can appeal against this decision. If not, it will ruin our business."

Herr Major made no effort to disguise a twisted smile, "By all means, but I must warn you that if the premises are not vacant by the time stated, there will be serious consequences."

With these chilling words, he brought the interview to an end, said, "Heil Hitler" and "Good day, Gentlemen."

That same morning, in Nathan's classroom, the teacher was taking down the names of those who wanted to join the Government's Hitler youth scheme. Nathan liked the sound of it. There would be healthy, outdoor team games, camping trips in the forest, the chance to learn woodcraft skills. They would be given brown uniforms to wear.

He put his hand up. He became aware that there was some sniggering and whispering from the blond boys behind him. He failed to notice that the two other Jewish boys in the class did not have their hands up.

At recess, a group of seven or eight boys began pushing him from one to the other, punching and kicking him every time he came within range, "Bloody Jew boy. You can't join the movement. Yids are not allowed."

The ringleader, an older boy called Franz Müller swung a punch at him. Soon they were wrestling on the ground, first one on top, then the other, fists flying. When Nathan seemed to be getting the better of it, the others pitched in to help their leader. Nathan was being kicked and punched from all directions. "Who's a lousy Jew boy? Who's a lousy Jew boy?" they were chanting in rhythm.

Two teachers passed nearby and Nathan shouted to them for help, but they looked away as if they had not heard.

Müller, now reasserting himself as leader said, "Let's teach this Jew boy a lesson he won't forget."

Two boys for each arm and leg, they carried him to a nearby tree. They tied his hands in front of him and then hoisted the rope over a low branch so that he had to stand on tiptoe to stop himself from

49

swinging. Amid screams of laughter, two of them roughly pulled down his shorts and underpants revealing his circumcised penis. As Müller approached, there were shouts of 'Cut them off, cut them off, cut them off...' and that was the last thing he heard before another punch to his face knocked him senseless and everything went black...

At the Grunfeld's office, the brothers barely had time to formulate their response to the Major's edict when Arthur was asked to take an urgent call from Ilse. Her voice was trembling and urgent, "Darling, come home at once. It's Nathan. He's badly hurt."

"Oh my God", gasped Arthur, "What's happened? Is he alright?"

"I can't tell. There's blood everywhere. Don't ask any more questions. Just come. Quickly."

CHAPTER 14

Arthur's hands were shaking so much that he could not fit the key in the door. Finally he rang the bell.

Ilse appeared at once, her eyes red with crying, "He's alright. He's alright..."

"Thank God," Arthur breathed.

They embraced.

"Doctor Lewin's coming over as soon as he can. He said just to let him sleep, if he can. Not to clean him up till he's been."

"So what happened?" asked Arthur as they went inside.

"He tried to join the Hitler Youth."

They went to his bedroom on tiptoe so as not to disturb him. The child's eyes were totally closed, swollen from heavy punching. His cheeks and chin were bright red from the blows and congealed blood. His nose had plasters running across it.

"Look at this," Ilse said as she gently lifted the blanket. His genitals had been painted in a thick, jet-black paint with big letters written across his abdomen: *JUDE.*

Arthur could contain his emotions no longer. He fell to his knees and began to cry loudly and unashamedly, his hands clasped in prayer, "Thank you, Dear God, for saving my son. My only son."

Thus reacts an atheist, in the moment of deep crisis – turning to God in desperation.

But Ilse appeared unmoved. She looked down at her husband with cold eyes, "Yes, Arthur, he feels so much like one of them, that he tries to join the Hitler Youth. Wonderful. Next stop, the SS."

When they had both calmed down, Arthur told of his interview with the Major, "If we close our head office, we might as well close the company," and, remembering the Major's twisted smile, "Perhaps that's what they want."

Ilse considered the option, "What if we ignore the order?"

"Doesn't bear thinking about. You know what I heard the other day? They are rounding up Jews, and shipping them down to a 'holiday camp' in Dachau just outside Munich. That could be us if we're not careful."

She was waiting for him to say the words that she wanted to hear more than any other. "Do you honestly think that we can stay here now?"

Arthur replied, "I think that things will get worse before they get better."

"You know what I think? For once, I believe every word that Hitler has said. I think that he will slowly exterminate all the Jews in Germany, either in camps or ghettos. I believe that all Jewish businesses will be closed down, the homes taken over, given to party members. To stay here and do nothing is to commit suicide. Better to leave with nothing and be alive than go to Dachau. We can already see the first step. Next it will be the house and then us. Can you honestly risk staying here and doing nothing? I beg you now, after what has happened today to leave. It's a sacrifice for all of us, of course it is, but it has to be."

Just then, the doorbell shrilled. Arthur saw a flame of fear leap in Ilse's eyes.

"Go look," she said, "make sure it's the doctor."

When the doctor had left, Arthur knelt by Nathan's bedside, "How are you feeling now, my little boy?"

"Better, thank you, Papa. Could I have a drink please?" his voice was drowsy.

Arthur picked up the glass of orange juice, placed a straw in it to help pass his lips and said, "Do you feel well enough to tell me just what happened at school today?"

Gradually, with stops and starts, Nathan told the full story.

"And were there no teachers? Did you not call out to them to help you?" asked Arthur, gently.

"I did," said Nathan, "I screamed out to them to help me... And they seemed to look.... though I could hardly see them because of the blood... But they must not have heard me... for just as I thought that I was saved... they seemed to look at one another and they turned away."

When Arthur went back downstairs, he said to Ilse, "Darling, you are right."

She fixed her solemn eyes upon him. "I would follow you to the end of the earth. Your decision is my decision. But, I honestly thank God that today's events have opened your eyes. We may not have long to wait before they take the house, then us."

When Walter arrived for a crisis meeting later that night, they calmly unfolded their plans. Walter had come to a similar conclusion. His wife, Inge, had relatives in America and they would settle there. Leaving everything behind them, they would pick up the Queen Elizabeth, sailing from Hamburg to New York.

Arthur would head for Manchester in England, where they had business contacts and friends who would help them to find their feet. They would take one of the factory vans, fill it with as much furniture as it would hold, drive through the night, through Germany and France, on to Calais, then to Dover and on to Manchester. The tricky bit would be crossing the border. They couldn't wait to be out of the Nazi clutches. A king's ransom, it would cost them, but worth every pfennig.

Said Arthur, "If we had the visas, we'd leave tomorrow."

"In that case..." said Ilse, walking to the bureau, she pulled out a wallet and brandished the three visas she had long ago secured. "In that case, Arthur, we leave tomorrow. We have the visas and I've been saving money for just this moment...."

He embraced her, "Darling, you are the most brilliant wife."

She replied, "Don't thank me. Thank my father."

CHAPTER 15

If Ilse was nervous on the day, she certainly didn't show it. There was feverish activity in the house as belongings were sorted into those being taken and those being left behind.

"Don't worry," Arthur said, "whatever we leave behind this time round, we'll pick up when we return. The blighters aren't going to be here forever."

Ilse was determined to leave the house spick and span, for fear that the next occupant might otherwise think badly of her.

"It's only going to be some damned Nazi," argued Arthur, "so who the hell cares?"

Arthur had arranged to meet Walter at the office for a final consultation. They emptied the safe and shared the contents out between them.

Arthur picked up about twenty samples, along with technical information for production purposes. He also sought the customer list, the autumn order books, shade cards, cashbook and Debtors List. If they couldn't run the business themselves, they were going to make sure that no one else could either. This was a sabotage operation and nothing was left behind that could be of any help to their successors.

Walter helped him load the two-ton truck, which they were to use for their escape. As they went back and forth, they considered whether to say a quiet farewell to any of their special staff with whom they had been friends, as well as colleagues. But they decided that total secrecy was important and that it would be best if they could reach their destination before being missed.

"I'd love to tell old Fassman he can have the design department now and do whatever he likes with it," Arthur said with a smile.

"He can have the whole company for that matter," Walter replied, "but I think he'll need more than one good eye to deal with it."

They had one final mission, a visit to the bank. Arthur collected the cheque-book, took a final look round the office and workroom from which they had conducted such a successful and happy operation, and with some sadness but much excitement, made his final exit.

They had decided to cash as big a cheque as it was possible without arousing suspicion. Walter had telephoned the manager beforehand telling him that they needed to buy a new machine, for which payment had to be in cash. They would collect the money early afternoon against a cheque, and wanted notes of the largest denomination. That would be fine, the bank manager agreed. Their mandate stipulated that both needed to sign cheques over the value of ten thousand marks, and their cheque carried both signatures.

The cashier studied the cheque, looked up the account and disappeared into one of the offices behind the counter. Five minutes later the manager, Peter Hartog came out, beckoned them to follow him into his office, "How are you both?" he asked effusively. "How nice to see you. Hard times these. Family well?" Small talk spoken as though no answers were expected. "The fact is, we have a bit of a problem here…"

"Problem…?" queried Walter, "but we're well within the limit."

"Indeed you are," he said, "it's not that at all." He lowered his voice,

"Earlier this week, the mandate was changed, requiring a third signature on every cheque."

"Third signature? Whose?"

"Well, I have it here," putting on his spectacles, "a Mr. Siegfried Fassman."

The brothers were shocked. Walter said, "But Mr. Fassman is a simple employee. He has no status, no shares; he's not even a Director. Who on earth gave him authority?"

"I'm afraid the mandate was given by an SS officer," again the glasses, "a Major Hans Wachtel." He continued, "They have the power, you know. I am sorry. I am sure Mr Fassman will be pleased to endorse the cheque. But I regret I cannot pay it without his signature."

Outside the bank, Walter, white with anger, said, "It's unbelievable. Our capital, our business, our expertise and that little shit gets the power to veto our cheques."

Arthur, a little calmer, said, "That's why we're getting out. Remember." He was tempted to go back to the office and collect more goods, but decided against. He had assembled quite enough key documents to enable him to carbon copy the Berlin operation in England whilst causing maximum disruption here. "Think, Walter, when Fassman tries to pick up the reins here... No samples, no films for the machines, no shade swatches, no order books. He won't even know what money they're owed. He'll be in a real mess. That idiot, Fassman may be signing cheques, but I bet that before long there will be nothing left to sign." They exchanged bitter smiles.

By 10 o'clock that night the van had been loaded with everything they were taking. Only the piano, cello and five gold chairs remained. Walter and his wife, Inge, had come to see them off. Ilse had prepared sandwiches, which they were enjoying with white wine. Nathan was still sore and stiff, but on his feet, and considered well enough to make the journey.

They were in the music room, where, over the years, they had spent so many happy hours. The walls were bare, the Renoirs having been carefully packed and strapped to the side of the van for safety. Without them, the room had lost its glow of warmth and colour.

Arthur was not prone to making speeches, but he felt that the occasion warranted a few words. "This, is a very sad day," he began. "And the end of an era. We have given up our home, our business, our way of life. And above all, it is the end of a wonderful partnership, so close, that it can only be enjoyed by brothers. Walter, we have had a great time together and I hope that one day a new W & A Grunfeld will rise from the ashes. And I hope that some day both W & A will be working together again. So I would like to propose a toast to the future. May it be as happy as the past?"

They drank and Walter responded in similar vein, saying how sad he was not to be going to England with them, but that they had been offered such a wonderful opportunity in America, which could not be missed. He said he hoped that one day they would be back to reclaim what they were leaving behind.

Arthur looked at his watch and picked up his cello. Ilse sat at the piano. He said, "Ilse and I would like to play in this room for one last time. It's a piece that we consider appropriate for the present time, and we would like to dedicate it to the thousands of Jews who are victims of Nazi oppression. *Kol Nidrei* by *Max Bruch*."

Of course the beauty of the music and solemnity of the occasion caused tears to flow from both performers and audience. As she began to play, Ilse's eyes locked with Arthur's. He looked his most handsome when playing – every bit the musician with film star qualities. And Arthur, when he looked at Ilse, saw the same natural girl with whom he had fallen in love when she had sung in the choir fourteen years before. He could barely take his eyes off her as they played in perfect unison. When it came to an end, they were all visibly moved. Their audience of three applauded.

Walter said, "That was wonderful, quite wonderful. You play........"

He choked with emotion and couldn't complete the sentence.

Nathan came to his rescue. "Please Mummy and Daddy, play the Beethoven. Please, please, please. I love it so much."

Arthur looked at his watch. Time was moving on. They had not intended to play more, but could hardly refuse. They knew exactly which Beethoven he wanted. It was the *Opus 69*, with its beautiful sonorous opening for cello solo.

Arthur said, "And this sonata we dedicate to the bravest young boy in the whole world. You are the joy of our lives and we love you."

It was a beautiful performance, which left players and audience on a high. They would have been so happy at this moment were it not for their imminent departure. Arthur and Ilse kissed. "You are a wonderful wife and a brilliant pianist. I will always love you," he said.

"And I you," she replied.

Ilse went upstairs to return with a little velvet bag in her hand. The piano was still open and she deftly unhooked six base strings, lifted the felt-topped hammers and placed the little bag beneath them, then stuck it to the side of the piano with tape, replaced the strings and stood back to admire her handiwork. Nothing was visible.

"Just in case some overzealous Nazi starts sniffing around for any valuables. I think that's pretty safe."

At college, they had taught Ilse how to dismantle a piano. This she now did with dexterity, and as the various components were detached, the brothers wrapped them in sacking and lifted them into the waiting van. As they came to the part containing the bag, Ilse said jokingly, "I'm watching you. Be careful."

By 11 o'clock they were ready to leave on their hazardous journey.

No one could restrain tears. The brothers embraced again and again. There were too many tears to say much. Arthur managed a little joke, "Try and drop in to see us when you're passing through."

Walter mopped his face with his handkerchief, picked up Nathan and hugging him said, "You are a credit to our family. You will grow up to be a fine man of integrity. After what you have been through, you will come out of it a strong person mentally and physically."

Nathan remembered these words all his life.

Now they just stood still for a minute or more as the tears ran unashamedly down their cheeks. No one said a word, yet everybody knew what was in their minds.

Finally Arthur said, "We have a long night ahead of us. We must get going."

Further tear-sodden embraces, as they climbed aboard the Mercedes van, waving till they lost sight as they drove off into the night.

CHAPTER 16

They aimed to hit the German/Dutch border town of Moers around midnight the following day. It was a distance of some eight hundred and fifty kilometres – a journey to be negotiated on small roads, some of which were in poor repair. They estimated that they would average fifty kilometres per hour, giving them only four hours sleep.

They passed Potsdam and Leipzig in good time then headed for Dortmund, which was about half way. There was a jangling of nerves as they saw the first signpost to Moers. They had chosen this border crossing as there was less likelihood of being confronted by any high-ranking Nazis. The strategy was to arrive just as the night shift was hoping to settle down for a quiet night and a discreet sleep.

They reached the town at about 10pm. Tension was high and they decided to wait until just after midnight before making their way to the border post.

The compound, when they approached it, was surrounded by barbed wire. Once inside, there was no way out. The barrier was opened, inviting them to drive in. The sentry on duty ordered them gruffly, "Bitte aussteigen."

Looking sheepish, all three of them emerged from the vehicle to be ushered into the immigration area. It was a primitive hut, with cross beams to support the roof. Large swastikas in black, white and red adorned the walls. The voice of Marlene Dietrich could be heard faintly from the radio at the back of the hut. Half-eaten sandwiches and a few bottles of Schnapps could be seen on the tables. Battle-dress jackets and helmets were hung on pegs at the side of the hut. Rifles stood in a stand nearby. This was a very relaxed outpost, clearly expecting no trouble and few travellers. Two SS men were playing cards as they entered. No one acknowledged them for five minutes.

Finally, when the hand was over, the younger of the two greeted them with a grudging, "Guten Abend."

Arthur, with a good-natured smile looked at his watch and replied, "Guten Morgen." Anything to break the ice.

The SS man smiled. "Your papers please."

Arthur handed over their identity cards, passports and exit visa. The officer studied them carefully as would a man without time restraints.

"Why are you leaving the Reich?"

"We are musicians. We have a concert tour planned for England and Scotland." Arthur continued… "My wife is a pianist and I play the cello."

"How long will you be away?"

"Maybe six months."

Casually, hoping to trap them – "Why is your visa out of date? It expired three months ago. I cannot let you through with this."

Ilse's heart sank. With all her preparations, she had overlooked getting the visa extended by a further six months. Arthur thought quickly, looked at Nathan, still a pitiful sight, and said in a low voice that only his interrogator could hear, "My son was ill, too ill to travel. I did not realise the visa had expired. He's a little better now. But three months ago, he could not have made it."

Arthur glanced at Ilse who was shaking visibly.

"You will have to go back to the 'Sicherheits Amt' where you received the visa in Berlin and obtain an extension."

"That would be disastrous. You see we have our first concert on Sunday night. We are the guests of Herr Von Ribbentrop, who has arranged a whole series of concerts in England to promote our great German composers."

This flagrant bit of name-dropping seemed to make an impression of which Arthur took advantage, "I am sure that if you were to telephone Herr Von Ribbentrop in London, he would vouch for us. He would be quite horrified if he thought his first concert, the most important of all, at the Albert Hall, had to be cancelled."

The young officer thought it a sufficiently plausible story, to seek further advice from his senior colleague. He took the papers over and was engaged in a lengthy conversation. Finally the older man, a colonel, came over. He must have been a war veteran. He was portly, had not a double, but more like a quadruple chin hanging down over his non-existent neck like a Christmas turkey.

"What are you playing at these concerts?" he asked, suspiciously.

"Herr von Ribbentrop wishes to demonstrate to the English people that our great German composers stand head and shoulders above any other. You could call it a cultural promotion to show that we Germans have music in our blood." He was laying it on a bit thick. Even Ilse thought that he was overdoing it.

"Which composers are you playing?"

"*Beethoven, Mozart, Haydn, Brahms.*"

"Ah so, nothing but the best. And what is the programme of your first concert?"

Arthur was not sure whether this was genuine interest or to test his story further, "*Beethoven and Haydn,*" he answered.

"Beethoven is the greatest."

"I share your opinion!"

"And what are you playing by *Beethoven and Haydn?*"

"We thought we would start with a flourish, so my beloved wife Ilse..." pointing to her, "is playing the Emperor."

"Wunderbar....wunderbar," said the Colonel and he burst into a spontaneous, very musical and pitch-perfect rendition of the last movement.

Arthur joined in conducting an imaginary orchestra. Ilse was nodding her head in time, just praying that they would not produce a piano from the back room and ask her to play from the concerto, which she had never studied. Arthur knew what she was thinking and, to take the pressure off her, said, "And I will be playing the *Second Haydn cello concerto.*"

Again the SS man burst into song with the main theme from the first movement.

"You have a very good knowledge of the classics," said Arthur trying to stop the vocal assault.

The situation was not without humour. Here was Arthur in an immigration hut, singing *Beethoven* and *Haydn* with the enemy. But, in spite of all the bonhomie and jovial chatter, the SS man was far from convinced. The Ribbentrop concerts really did sound fishy. He sought further proof. "You will have your cello with you?"

"In the van."

"It would make a lovely interlude if you would play for us a little."

Arthur was a showman. He would play for anyone, anywhere – but for the Nazis in an immigration hut at two in the morning? – This was bizarre beyond measure. But, by God, thought Arthur, if this will help us get out, so be it.

The cello had been loaded last, so that it was easy to retrieve. He was offered a chair, took the cello from its case, tuned it by ear and then began to play the opening theme of the first movement of the Haydn cello concerto. The room became very still as the strains of the music swelled. The colonel was like a man hypnotised. Once Arthur saw that he had his audience rapt, he began to extemporise variations with the artistry of a master, before returning to the original melody. He finished with a flourish, his bow in the air. He had played for about five minutes. It was a quite brilliant performance.

The colonel applauded vigorously, "Music has no barrier," he said, "That was superb. Thank you for making the night shift so lively." He turned away and spoke to his junior colleague, anxious to reassert his power, and then came back to Arthur and Ilse, "We are prepared to overlook the invalid exit visa, but will need to examine the contents of the van and yourselves in compliance with regulations."

There then followed a meticulous search to check if any valuables were being smuggled out. Ilse had taken the precaution of wearing only a cheap gold ring on her wedding finger without diamonds. The real one was in the velvet bag within the piano.

"Do you have any other jewellery?" asked the SS man.

"No," Ilse lied, hoping that her blushes would not give her away.

They were then asked to drive the van into a floodlit bay, where the two guards under the supervision of the young officer, unloaded the van of all its contents, except for the piano, and proceeded to inspect each item with meticulous precision. Ilse's heart was thumping hard, for fear they would go back into the van to examine the piano. Mercifully, no such thing happened, because they had found something much more interesting.

They reloaded the van with everything but the Renoirs. These, they took back into the building for the colonel's inspection.

"I see you have nice paintings by Renoir. I love the Impressionists," the Colonel said affably.

He picked up the phone and had a lengthy conversation. Ilse and Arthur could not hear with whom but, in retrospect, thought it might have been with Reichsmarshal Göring himself, or his aide. Finally, the colonel turned to them and said, "We regret that Reich regulations do not permit the export of any works of art. I therefore have to inform you officially, that these paintings must remain in Germany. I will give you a receipt and you may reclaim them when you return to this country."

Ilse eyed him sceptically. But Arthur smiled thinking that the Colonel's reference to 'returning to this country' indicated that their ordeal might soon be over.

The Colonel's retirement was not far distant and it had been his brief to train his young inexperienced second-in-command how to deal effectively with these Jews as they tried to leave the country. Here was a good opportunity to prove his authority. He called over the young officer, who was on the point of enjoying a glass of schnapps, and whispered, "Schultz, I think these people are telling us a pack of lies." He clicked his heels in the first show of military discipline.

"Jawohl, Herr Colonel, I think so too."

Gone was the affable, music-loving, smiling Colonel. He stretched to his full height, and with considerable gravity addressed Arthur and Ilse jointly, "Perhaps you would be kind enough to explain to me how it is that you are going to England for six months on a concert tour and are taking with you enough belongings and furniture to settle there for good."

Arthur began, "Herr Colonel, you will understand these are very unsettled times we live in at the moment. We have left most of our belongings at our home in Berlin. These few things we have taken with us are to allow us to be comfortable when we arrive in England. We are performing artists. We need our comforts."

"Oh yes," replied the Colonel, his chin shaking as he spoke, "you need your Renoirs to be comfortable," with icy sarcasm, "very comfortable indeed."

Arthur replied calmly, "We had intended to give one to our friend

Herr Von Ribbentrop in appreciation of his help in arranging the tour. And to let him choose which he likes best."

This seemed to anger him. There was nothing affable about him now.

"You will wait here until morning, when I will speak with the Ambassador."

Ilse exerted her feminine charms, "Please understand, Herr Colonel, that we have our first concert in two days' time and have to rehearse the day before. If we are delayed here until tomorrow, we will miss the rehearsal and maybe the concert. All those people will be disappointed."

"I have made my decision. We will see in the morning." With that, he indicated that the interview was at an end and motioned Schultz to retire from the conversation. He patted him on the back and could just be heard to say, "You see, Schultz, that is the way to handle these people."

The Grunfelds could do nothing but sit, wait and watch. They could see the Colonel on the telephone. He seemed to be talking endlessly. When dawn broke, he was still talking. Arthur could see that he was looking hard at one of the Renoirs.

Nathan was shivering more from fright than cold and the Nazis offered him a blanket in which he sat huddled, his shoulders drooping.

He looked a pathetic sight with his battered face, black eye and split lip.

They were all concerned at what might happen if and when the office of Von Ribbentrop was contacted. Would they be arrested for their fabrication, or allowed to go back to Berlin? It was the longest and hardest five- hour wait that they had ever endured. Arthur recalled how angry the Colonel had been when told that the Ambassador could choose one of the Renoirs. Could it be jealousy? Could he be angling for one of the pictures for himself? Suppose he could get the Colonel on his own and find out? They were going to lose them anyway, so it didn't really matter which of the Nazis had them.

Arthur was watching the Colonel carefully. He waited for the telephone conversation to end, then sauntered casually to his desk, asked the Colonel in a low voice whether he could have a discreet word with him. Not so much as a nod, but a grunt of acquiescence. The Colonel looked to his left to observe Schultz dozing lightly at his desk, his head lolling forward, seemingly detached from his body. The Colonel lit a cigarette and contemptuously blew a cloud of smoke into Arthur's face, with no word of apology. "What is it?" he asked, gruffly.

Arthur's hope was to get him back to their common interest, "I was wondering, does the Colonel play an instrument?" he asked with feigned humility.

The Colonel was unwilling to be drawn into a conversation when he was tired and near the end of his shift. He muttered, "I play the piano – not well."

Arthur was encouraged to have got a response, "I can tell from your singing that you are a fellow musician."

The Colonel fell for the flattery. Arthur took advantage, "I will tell you something interesting Colonel, if you will allow me. My music room at home in Berlin has a Renoir facing the piano. When we make music, we look at it all the time. Can you believe that, in a subconscious way, it is an inspiration to us to match the beauty of the picture with the quality of our performance?" He sighed deeply at the memory and continued with conviction. "It is as though music and art – the sense of seeing and hearing feed off one another. It is like magic."

The Colonel said, "I can imagine that might be so. If you have the good fortune to have a Renoir to look at....."

Arthur could not have wished for a better opening. Having enjoyed such success with his earlier compliment, he repeated it, "I can see you are indeed a fellow musician. In the name of Music, I would like you to experience the same inspiration that my wife and I enjoy in our music making."

The Colonel was wide awake now. He stubbed out his cigarette and cleared the smoke with his hand.

"How can that be possible?"

"I would be happy for you to have one of our Renoirs – as a gift."

The Colonel's face was transformed. He beamed with pleasure and shook Arthur's hand in gratitude, "That is very kind of you indeed," he said, "Which one do you suggest I have?"

Arthur thought this a bit much: not only giving but picking as well. He said, "It's your choice, whichever you love the most."

The Colonel's craggy face relaxed into a beatific smile. He picked up each of the masterpieces in turn and looked longest at his favourite. Moments later, the receipt for the pictures had been rewritten by the Colonel, omitting any reference to the retention of a painting called 'La Seine.'

The documentation was duly completed and the visa stamped 'Approved.'

The Colonel personally escorted them to their van and wished them 'Bon Voyage.'

Once out of the compound, they cheered aloud. "Thank you, Herr von Ribbentrop, here we come," said Arthur.

Ilse replied, "How on earth did you manage that?"

Once across the border into Holland, Arthur, Ilse and Nathan got out of the van. They threw their arms around each other, laughing in thankful relief.

"Thank God it worked. I talked such rubbish," said Arthur. "We've paid a heavy price – but saved by the Renoirs."

"It could have been a lot worse," said Ilse philosophically, "they missed the one that was taped to the side, behind the piano."

She got into the back of the van, crawled over the contents to establish which one it was that the Nazis had left behind. She returned with a big smile on her face, "It's 'The Two Girls at the Piano.' My favourite. I am so happy."

They breathed in deeply. The air in Holland was so much cleaner.

CHAPTER 17

Manchester in 1936 was very different from Berlin – set back in the past and underdeveloped. One dingy, decrepit mill next to another with smoking chimneys polluting the air. It looked to the Grunfelds like relics of the Industrial Revolution, a poverty-stricken area of working class people. Yet working they were. Thousands of them could be seen early in the morning on foot, bicycle or trams, cramming into the antiquated factories and office buildings. The men all looked the same as they rushed to clock in on time. Cloth cap or soft-brimmed bowler, a collar-less shirt, ill-fitting jacket and baggy trousers seemed to be the regular work gear.

At the end of the day, the focus became the public houses, which were plentiful. From six o'clock onwards these were full of patrons, inside and out, drinking, smoking, talking.

There seemed little opportunity here for any cultural pursuits. Music Hall seemed to be the only type of live performance, which was flourishing – several theatres were in competition with one another, to attract patrons away from the pubs. Once Arthur spotted a billboard advertising the *Hallé Orchestra*, which provoked the thought of joining. But no, he must push ahead with the plan.

The Grunfelds socialised little for, though they spoke reasonable English, they found it very difficult to follow the accent. Indeed it was like another language, quite different to the one they had learnt at school.

But the most strikingly wondrous difference was that they could walk the streets without fear. No furtive glances around street corners to check if there were any Nazis lurking. No jackbooted bully-boys to dodge. No 'no go' areas to avoid. Not a day passed without them expressing eternal gratitude that their host nation had offered them security free of racial hatred.

Arthur's friend and sponsor in Manchester was a very well-connected Mancunian by the name of Willie Ullman. He was not only an astute businessman, but also a highly respected figure in the Jewish community. The two company chairmen had met at a Fashion Fair in Berlin some years before and had since forged strong business links, discussing how they could use their respective sales forces and designs to mutual advantage. Negotiations had been at an advanced stage by the time Hitler came to power. Their dialogue had then taken on a different tack. Would it be possible to move the Grunfeld operation to Manchester until the Hitler crisis blew over? In this moment of crisis, Willie Ullman proved himself to be a true friend with an astute brain and a good eye for an outstanding deal.

He had an empty mill, which could convert well enough into producing knitwear. They negotiated an equal partnership, with Grunfelds having total autonomy. Ullman would provide the premises, Grunfelds the expertise. They would each put up ten thousand pounds to set up and run the company. Salaries would only be paid to the operators, but profit would be shared equally by the partners.

Willie proved himself to be more than a friend and partner. It was he who found their first home, a small but pleasant house in Didsbury, a nearby Manchester suburb, at the rent of two pounds per week, which he had paid three months in advance.

Ilse busied herself with making it into a home and it was not long before things were reasonably ship-shape with a nice alcove for the piano, with the Renoir, its constant companion, above it.

Willie was an early visitor. The unfamiliar vowels of his accent made communication diffficult. "Well mah friends, ah thought ah'd look in – see you're coomf'table. Ah know Didsbury's not what you're used to. An' Manchester's no Berlin, eether. But we look after's own here, joost th' same." Ilse could understand him a little better than Arthur. She said, "Willie, you have been so wonderful. I don't know what we do here without your help." He put his arm around her. "Mah pleasure. N' 'ow's th' lad?" he enquired, looking at Arthur. "Na-athan, 'en'it. Mah own lad seems t'get on all reet wi' 'im at school. An' mah nephews. 'Ow's 'e getting' on wi' his English?" Arthur could barely follow. "Better than me, Willie, I think." "Aye, well," he continued, "don't f'get, if he wants t'join the

Schul or think 'bout havin' a Bar Mitzvah, joost let me know. Or mention mah name to the Chazen. They all know Willie Ullman round 'ere. Soomtahms I wish'd they didn't." He chuckled at the thought of his notoriety. "But what about you Arthur. When're y'coomin' t'see th'mill?"

"That's what I wanted to talk about Willie."

"What's on y'mind?" Arthur took him to one side and chose his words carefully from his limited vocabulary. "You have been such a kind and good friend to me and my family, I do not like to ask another favour." Willie waved his hand dismissively. Arthur continued, "well my position is diffficult. Would you permit me to place my ten thousand after yours? I need about three months when my money will arrive."

Without hesitation, Willie replied, "Mah good friend, y'don't have t'ask. Take six months even longer if y'need it. Mah ten thou'll start's off, coover cost of machines and settin'oop. Ah'm sure your share'll be available when mine roons out."

Arthur was visibly moved by this generous offer. "How can I ever thank you?"

Willie patted him on the back, "Y' doan't 'ave to. This is Manchester. And ah'm a Jew. And yoo're a Jew. It's mah great pleasure to help. And don't f'get, ah'll be expectin' to ma-ake some good brass, oonce y'get full potential from th'factory."

When Arthur saw the empty mill for the first time, he was shocked. It must have stood empty for an eternity. He could not imagine that anything ever had nor ever would or could, take place in that terrible building. It comprised three stories, must have been about twenty thousand square feet in all. There was no light. Cobwebs brushed against their faces as they trod carefully over the rubbish-strewn floor. The beam of the torch revealed bats hanging off the timbers, which took flight, disturbed by their intrusion. Arthur swore he could feel rats running over his feet. He could not wait to get out. As they emerged into the light, he said, "For me, there is too much wildlife in there!"

Willie brushed the cobwebs from his face and jacket. Apologetically he explained, "Last time I were 'ere, it were a smasher; but tha' were fifteen years back. But leave it to me, Arthur. Ah'll get mah work force down 'ere. In three weeks, y'won't recognise it for same place, I promise you." Arthur thought of his lovely factory in Berlin. Would he ever be able to work in these conditions?

Three weeks later, he returned to find the place transformed. The floor had been screeded and was smooth to walk on; the walls and ceiling smelt of fresh paint. New windows had been installed which were open, allowing fresh air to ventilate. There was no sign of bats, rats or any other creatures. Arthur immediately saw the potential, "Willie, it is incredible what you have done. It is now a place we can work successfully. It will be excellent. We use only the ground floor for now and when we get bigger, we go upstairs."

He set about planning the layout of his knitting machines and drew a sketch of what would go where. This was exciting. The new W. & A Grunfeld was about to grow from the ashes of the old.

The news from Berlin was alarming. The position had deteriorated sharply. Jews were being pulled from their homes, sometimes by their beards, tortured or killed. Property was smashed, then set alight, bonfires lit, burning Jewish works of art and belongings. Even printed books by Jewish writer Heinrich Heine and music by Jewish composer Felix Mendelsohn were considered corrupt and burnt in public. A Jew under attack had nowhere to run. Find the Police and they'd laugh in your face and join the tormentors. And the more they killed and looted, the greater the shouts of encouragement. Then they had to contend with identification. All Jews were ordered to show a gold Star of David on their jacket. Wear it and you were doomed. Hide it and you were dead, if caught.

As they heard the news, Ilse said, "Thank God we're here. I am so looking forward to starting the business."

They had discussed it many times. It was arranged that Ilse would work with her husband to launch the company. With this in mind, Arthur had been in a quandary for some days. How do you ask your wife to give up her most treasured possession? He began, fumbling for the right words, but need not have bothered. Ilse came to his rescue at once. "You don't have to say it, Arthur. I am not a child. We came here with nothing and need to raise ten thousand pounds for our stake. Our net assets are my jewellery, clothes we stand up in and one Renoir. It will hurt a lot to lose any of my pieces or the picture, but it has to be. It is more important to rebuild the business than to satisfy our ego with things of beauty. We have to hope that the future will bring us enough money to replace whatever we sell. We have to do it. Take whatever you will to raise the money. Don't even tell me about it. I don't want to hear. Just do it".

These were easy words but, when Ilse sat at the piano, she was looking at only the rim of dust where the beautiful Renoir had hung.

CHAPTER 18

Mr. Pettigrew appeared from behind the reception counter and with a knowing smile said, "Nice of you to come to see us, Mr. Grunfeld." He was very effete in dress and manner, wearing an orange cravat, secured by a be-jewelled pin, and a grey double-breasted pin stripe suit with a carefully matched nasturtium flower in his buttonhole.

He took Arthur through to a small room nearby. Arthur undid the package and presented the masterpiece with pride. Mr Pettigrew examined it with meticulous care from afar. Then scrutinised some of the detail through a collapsible magnifying glass that he produced from his inside pocket. He studied the signature and date, 1894, in total silence. Finally, considering his words carefully, he said, "There is much demand and interest in the work of this artist. It is a very special and pleasing painting, as nice as any I have seen by this artist. I feel that you will secure the best price by offering it for sale by auction". Impressionists had been enjoying a good run of late. A Monet had achieved a record price of eleven thousand pounds.

"What sort of figure can we expect?"

"It is always difficult to forecast, depending on who is in the room and what sort of competition there is to purchase. Taking all things into account, I would recommend a guide price of eight to twelve thousand pounds, and a reserve of seven thousand, although this should be flexible and be decided on the day of the auction."

They discussed terms and fixed the auction date for six weeks later.

Arthur left Sotheby's with an overwhelming pang of conscience. Had he done the right thing? But he told himself, 'We need the money too badly now to be sentimental.'

CHAPTER 19

The knitting machines were due to arrive. Their installation would signal the start of their operation in earnest. Arthur had engaged a refugee from Hungary, Lotzi Papp, to run the machines. What Lotzi didn't know about knitting wasn't worth knowing.

A crane gently lowered the giant machines to their allotted space and one by one Lotzi nursed them into action.

Ever since he had left Berlin, Arthur had been looking forward to the moment he could write to his former customers. This he now did, with some relish:

"A Special Announcement"
Dear esteemed customer,
W. & A. Grunfeld has moved its operation to Manchester in England. The Directors could not condone the hostile political situation and found it necessary to re-locate in a more sympathetic environment.
The same Directors and technicians that have always guaranteed high quality are with us and we are hoping that you will be prepared to accept deliveries from us in the future as in the past.
Our Spring range is in preparation with the same designer expertise we have always shown and we look forward to its presentation. W.& A. Grunfeld of Manchester is at your disposal and we look forward to continuing our association with you.
Yours sincerely,
Arthur and Ilse Grunfeld.

Letters of support from former customers were encouraging. One particularly pleased them – it stated that the Grunfeld plant in Berlin had closed, and that no orders would be delivered. '*And even if they were*', the letter continued, '*we would not accept their deliveries, knowing that you are operating in England.'*

The day of the Sotheby's auction arrived. Arthur had planned his schedule to attend. Ilse was in two minds whether or not to go. On the one hand she wanted to see for herself how it went and have a final glimpse of the painting she so loved. On the other, it would be heartbreaking to see ownership passed on. In the end, curiosity got the better of her and because Arthur promised her a lovely day as well, they set off together.

They arrived at Euston with at least three hours to spare before Lot 34 was due to go under the hammer and, since it was a lovely day, they decided to walk to the gallery, taking in on the way the stores that they must target as potential customers for their product.

London was very relaxed at the time. War clouds were far distant. The fashionable ladies were casually dressed in summer clothes with short-sleeved blouses and full, long dirndl skirts.

It took them several minutes to cross Oxford Circus, where the two-way traffic was fast and noisy. The double-decker buses with their spiral stairway were in no hurry to let them cross. So they waited patiently. There was no rush.

They studied the windows at Peter Robinson with interest, then walked down Oxford Street to Marshall & Snelgrove. Arthur said, "We should certainly target these two stores. Our product is perfect for them."

They took a right turn to have a look at Debenham & Freebody. This was of special interest to Arthur since they had supplied the store from Germany. They went in and asked to meet their contact buyer, a Miss Enid Wright.

She was sitting at an ornate desk in the middle of the department. A petite lady with long greyish hair, plaited and piled on top of her head. She gave them a warm welcome, more than interested to hear that their merchandise could now be obtained from England.

"Wonderful," she said, "I'll be saving all that duty and show a higher mark-up." It emerged that Debenham & Freebody did a large part of their turnover by catalogue. She suggested that the Grunfeld merchandise would be featured in depth together with a profile of the company.

They were so excited about the project and the ideas that stemmed from it, that they completely forgot the reason for their trip to London. Suddenly Arthur looked at his watch and saw to his horror that they had only ten minutes before their lot would come up.

They ran all the way down Bond Street, holding hands, to reach Sotheby's out of breath with only minutes to spare. They rushed up the stairs to find the room packed with people, standing six deep in the doorway and on the aisles. The best they could do was to find two standing places at the side from which they could see the easel and watch the auctioneer.

They barely had time to take in their surroundings. A rectangular room, open ended at the back, where the crowds were thickest. Little gold chairs in rows all occupied, facing the podium where the auctioneer, with various assistants at his side, was conducting proceedings. The walls were heavily adorned with pictures, some of which they recognised from the catalogue.

"At least we've got a full house," said Arthur.

"I'm nervous. Is it too late to withdraw?" Ilse asked.

"I would say yes, we're only two lots away."

Ilse's heart was thumping. She had to look away when her beloved Renoir was placed on the easel. My best friends in the whole world, she thought, these two lovely girls with long hair sitting at the piano. How could I do this to them? It was too much for her. She squeezed Arthur's hand, which was damp with nervous perspiration.

"And now a very fine Renoir from the artist's most prolific period, dated 1894. Who will start the bidding?"

Silence. No response.

"Good", whispered Ilse, "We can take it back home where it belongs."

"Will anyone start me off at two thousand pounds?"

A solitary hand went up. Ilse knew that they were safe up to seven thousand; the reserve agreed the previous day. The bidders had a long way to go and seemed to be reluctant. Maybe they'd get away with it and take the picture home…

"Thank you, Sir", said the auctioneer. "Two thousand pounds I am bid. Anyone for two and a half…"

A lady obliged and that started the ball rolling. Two thousand five hundred… three thousand… three thousand five hundred … four thousand....

The auctioneer began to jump in increments of a thousand - he was gaining confidence by the number of bids he was receiving. Six thousand... six thousand five hundred... But now there was a pause. He needed one more bid to reach the reserve and then he would sell. The lady obliged with a further bid.

Ilse let out a sigh and sat back. The reserve was reached. Ilse looked at Arthur with mixed emotions. They both realised the significance. But now the casual bidders had been left behind and a battle developed. From seven to eight thousand to nine to ten thousand, eleven, twelve, thirteen, fourteen thousand.

Arthur could hardly believe it. Surely, no work of art could be worth so much. Ilse had now accepted she would never see it again and now was hoping it might even make twenty thousand.

There was still a lot of steam left in the bidding...fifteen thousand, sixteen thousand, seventeen thousand, eighteen thousand, nineteen thousand. Then a pause, but the gentleman on the left wearing a jacket with a velvet collar, made a further bid.

The Auctioneer now bristled with confidence. "I have twenty thousand pounds. Will anyone give me twenty-one? Your last chance, I will sell at twenty, going, going…"

He was interrupted by a new bidder, who shouted, "Five hundred pound..."

"I will accept twenty thousand five hundred. Against you, Sir."

The first bidder came up with another five hundred, but one could sense that this might be the end of him. The late bidder raised his hand again, unwisely leaving the increment to the auctioneer who was quick to take advantage.

"I am bid twenty-two thousand. Any more bids? Have you all done? For the last time going…going… " The hammer came down, "To the gentleman at the back of the room." He continued, "This is the highest recorded price for an Impressionist painting. Thank you."

Ilse could not make up her mind whether to laugh or cry. Fearing the latter, Arthur put his arms around her, "What a wonderful price. Now we'll have enough capital left to buy a home."

He could see tears coming, so he joked. "Old Mr. Templeman knew what he was talking about, when he said they were going up in price every day."

But Ilse was scarcely listening. She had only one thought in mind
– how and when she could get the painting back.

CHAPTER 20

Just as a chameleon changes its colour to blend with its surroundings, so it was with Nathan. He became anglicised very quickly and was quite obsessed with any activity that appertained to his new home in Manchester.

Willie was an ardent supporter of Manchester United Football club, and travelled with the team wherever they might be playing. When Willie offered Nathan a seat in his box at Old Trafford, he was thrilled and became an enthusiastic fan, missing not a single home match all season. Of course he got to know all the players by name and was soon shouting advice and encouragement to the players, as if his life depended upon their success.

When Nathan came home from the match elated, he found his mother crying in the music room. Since the sale of the painting, she had become morose and depressed. She could bring herself to do nothing. She did not speak to anyone. Arthur and Nathan had done their utmost to console her, but they found her to be inconsolable. *The Two Girls at the Piano* had always been her favourite and now it was as though she had lost her dearest friends.

Nathan had an idea. There was an art gallery nearby, at which he often stopped to look at pictures on display. He had never been inside until today. His inexperienced eye took in all the pictures at a glance. There were no Renoirs or other impressionists to his dismay. But his attention was riveted by three pictures in an alcove. He went up close. It was a large picture he liked best. This was the very Manchester scene that they had observed so often. People, hundreds of them, all rushing to work. There were big factories with tall smoking chimneys. The background was dull grey-white and the colourful clothing worn by the little characters was vivid against it.

Nothing like the Renoir, but Manchester was their new home and

Nathan felt very akin to his new surroundings. He was quite taken by the beauty of the picture, its movement, colour and three-dimensional aspect. He noticed the suggestion of another large town in the background with yet more chimneys and factories. He thought it a very exciting picture. He asked the lady in the gallery timidly who the painter was.

"Its only a local artist, dear," she replied, "Called Lowry, Laurence Stephen Lowry. He's such a nice man. Comes in every month with some new pictures and we usually pick two or three. Always wears a grey suit with a black tie. We always say, 'Mr. Lowry, you've got more paint on your suit than on the picture.' We give him a cup of tea, bless him, and he always stays for a chat."

"How much is the *Industrial Scene*?" Nathan asked.

"Can you manage five pounds love?"

Ilse didn't know what to say or think when Nathan unwrapped his purchase. She was touched by the lovely gesture... but this, to replace her Renoir?...hardly. Nonetheless, they hung it over the piano in the now vacant space.

"Mother, it's Manchester as we see it every day. Look at the distant factories just in outline and the big ones in the foreground." Then pointing to the white sky, "How can any painter produce that effect, I love it so much."

Ilse had never before seen her son so enthusiastic about a painting and so as not to dampen his enchantment, she said, "It really is very nice. Thank you so much darling. A lovely thought. What are those funny figures doing, and so many of them?" Still gazing... "It does have impact. You couldn't walk into the room and not notice it. It just takes a bit of getting used to it, after the Renoir. I am sure it will grow on me with time."

When Arthur got home, the first thing he saw was the enormous new painting, hanging over the piano. "What on earth is that?" he demanded.

Ilse nudged him, requesting diplomacy. "Nathan bought it for me. It's really lovely, don't you think?"

"My first reaction is shock. All those funny little people, what on earth are they doing?"

Ilse murmured, sotto voce, "Careful what you say. Nathan is besotted with it. He loves anything that is Manchester."

"There's a lot of movement," he said, "that's for sure, but is this art?" And under his breath, "Fine if the boy likes it, but couldn't we hang it somewhere a little less prominent?"

CHAPTER 21

September 3rd 1939. Arthur and Ilse were sitting around the radio in the lounge awaiting a statement from Neville Chamberlain. The time was 11 o'clock.

Germany, with all its might, had moved into Poland, with whom England and France had a non-aggression alliance. 'Attack Poland', the politicians of both countries had said, 'and you attack us.' Hitler had ignored these threats and unleashed a savage attack on its comparatively defenceless neighbour. Chamberlain had demanded an undertaking from Hitler for an immediate cessation of hostilities, with an ultimatum that expired at 11am that day.

The Prime Minister's statement was bland, "We have received no such undertaking and we are therefore in a state of war with Germany."

No one can celebrate a declaration of war. The implications are too horrific. But German Jewish refugees, who knew the strength of the Nazi hold over the German people, realised that only an international coalition could crush the Nazi regime. From within, there was no chance. From without, it would require overwhelming power to defeat Hitler's highly trained, Army, Luftwaffe and Navy, all of which had been building in strength since 1933.

Up to this point, the fortunes of W & A Grunfeld had been encouraging. The first year had shown a loss as expected, but the following year there was a small profit, leading to an excellent result the year after. It looked as though they were heading for a profit of around sixty thousand pound in the current year. Arthur took great pride in writing the company's first cheque in favour of Willie Ullman and said, "Writing a cheque can be a painful business sometimes, but this one gives enormous pleasure, and I hope it will be the first of many." He put a friendly arm around Willie and continued, "We have built a great partnership, you and I, and I cherish our friendship more than ever and always will."

The two upper floors had by now been refurbished, since the expanding business now needed every square foot of space that it could get. Ilse made a superb job of developing the relationship with Enid Wright of Debenham & Freebody. The catalogue with its splendid profile on Grunberg knits, had proved a huge success, which other West-End stores were keen to follow. Ilse had developed a skilful mix of business and pleasure by taking the buyers to fashionable restaurants and the odd show to cement the friendship. A London presence was now needed badly, and a modest showroom was opened at 13 Berners Street, so that buyers from all over the world could see the Grunfeld products.

By now Lotzi's machines were turning twenty-four hours a day and exceeding production targets week by week. Most manufacturers found it difficult to purchase fabric, for which coupons were introduced. The only raw product Grunfeld required was yarn and this continued to be available from the spinning mills in Yorkshire. And as the dearth of fashion goods made itself felt, it was to the advantage of those who could produce and deliver. Grunfelds fell into this category.

Nathan was left very much to his own devices, while his parents were building the business; but they were very aware that he was not enjoying his school. He was branded a 'Kraut' and had to fight his way through the curriculum with tough Mancunian youths, who could not, or would not, comprehend that, as a German Jew, he had more reason to hate the Germans than they did. To them, a 'Kraut' was a 'Kraut'. The gangs would lie in wait for him the moment he arrived, rough him up, taunt him with 'out Kraut'. If he attempted to run away, it would inevitably lead to a dogfight.

Often, he would sit through class nursing a split lip or bleeding nose and was more concerned with planning his escape after the lesson than paying attention to the subject matter. He was not a natural scholar anyway, but the continued harassment meant that his performance was well below par. He found it difficult to follow the language, let alone the dialect.

The school was very proud of its sporting prowess. Had he been cricket or rugby material, his passage would have eased considerably, but he had no such fortune. He was quite averse to any sports activity and when it came to compulsory cross-country running, he would arrive with a note from home, asking to be excused for one reason or another. So the first year of school was very distressing. He would look forward to the sanctuary of his home and the comforting embrace of his mother who listened to his problems patiently. She would help him with his homework, since very often he could not understand what was required of him.

"It's just too bad for the poor boy," she said to Arthur in the evening, "In Germany he gets beaten up because he's Jewish. In England he gets it because he's German. Can't those idiots realise that it is our right to hate the Germans more than anyone."

Becoming very introverted and always on the defensive, Nathan turned to the Jewish community at the Synagogue. It was a place where ideas and thoughts could be exchanged freely, and friendships forged. For a young man of thirteen, not yet shaving, he had a remarkable understanding of world affairs and with his first-hand experience of German brutality he was well placed to explain the power and ambitions of the Nazi regime.

He was also very knowledgeable on matters pertaining to music. He came into contact with a music professor of middle age, by name of Richard Appleby, with whom he shared a similar taste in classics. They spent many hours, his happiest, in mutual quizzing of Beethoven themes for which Nathan had an impressively retentive memory. He sang them, showing great musicality and a well articulated voice of unusual clarity. He had a fine treble voice, not yet broken and could read music better than most. Richard was working on a performance of The Messiah and thought it would be an excellent idea for Nathan to join the choir. His parents were over-joyed at this development.

For all his singing ability, his piano playing left much to be desired. He had regular lessons, but was never going to get anywhere. Every piece he played was learnt by brute force. Bar for bar, hands separately, a hundred times over, before it clicked and even then, he could be guaranteed a high percentage of wrong notes and discord. Frequently, Arthur held his hands over his ears as Nathan produced fearful sounds from their beautiful Bechstein. But Ilse would sit with him for hours patiently hoping for progress that never really came.

Willie Ullman meanwhile, had arranged Nathan's Bar Mitzvah. Arthur and Ilse were very proud of their son, as he spoke the prayers with confidence. Although he still looked young, he was beginning to show signs of early manhood.

Looking at Nathan in his best suit, Ilse thought how handsome he was, just like his father. He was growing his thick, brown wavy hair a little longer for the occasion and often ran his fingers through it, brushing it back from his forehead. He had recently become aware of his charms and was starting to use it to great advantage. He seemed to be a little shorter than his contemporaries, but was developing a lively, humorous personality.

Ilse was reminded of what her brother-in-law, Walter used to say, "Take all the shit the world can throw at you as a kid, and you'll grow up to be a stronger and better man."

When the Grunfelds had moved into their spacious new home in Hale, Nathan was allocated a self-contained flat to himself on the top floor, with a free hand to furnish and decorate as he chose. Arthur, forever conscious of fixing a not-to-be-exceeded budget, set the figure at two hundred pounds.

Nathan went back to the little gallery in Didsbury to see if he could buy some more Lowrys. The lady remembered him at once from his previous visit and directed him to the same alcove on which were displayed three new paintings by his favourite artist. He would have liked to buy all three, but had only ten pounds to spend. The one he liked best was called *Children's Playground*, which had a lot of happy children queuing up for swings, slides and round-abouts. The wonderful crusty white sky, the first thing Nathan looked for, was there, and he considered this to be a very cheerful and optimistic picture. He was surprised to hear that the price had gone up to twenty pounds, which he worked out was an increase of four hundred percent.

"The last one was only five pounds," he said.

"That was a few years ago, love," she answered. "He's become quite popular since then, and now, I have a few clients collecting them."

"I only have ten pounds on me. Could I come back with the other ten pounds later?"

"I'm sure that Mr. Lowry wouldn't mind that, seeing that you are a regular buyer of his work."

"Would there be any chance of meeting him when he comes to see you next time?"

"I don't think that would be quite right. You see, Mr. Lowry is a very private person."

What she really had in mind was that it wasn't good business practice to introduce artists to clients, for fear they might bypass the gallery in future and buy direct. Nathan had to wait until the first ever Lowry one-man-show was staged before he could meet his idol. At the show, he bought another picture called *Street Scene*, but had to tackle his parents for fifty pounds to pay for it.

Mr. Lowry seemed a very pleasant and ordinary person with a strong Northern accent. He did not look at all like an artist and, were it not for the splotches of paint on his hands and jacket, one would not have associated him with anything artistic. Wearing a black tie, unevenly tied and a crumpled, tatty jacket, he looked quite out of place in an art gallery.

Nathan overcame his nerves and approached him, "I've got two of your pictures already, Mr. Lowry, and I'm buying a third. I really love them."

"Thank you very much young man," replied the painter, "I'm happy that you like 'em. You must be one of my youngest collectors."

Nathan took a catalogue from the display table, held it out with the blank page on its back cover uppermost, "Would you mind giving me your autograph?"

With a felt pen, Mr Lowry drew three figures standing outside a house, added a couple of dogs and signed it L.S.L. It took him less time to sketch than to describe. It was, in its simplicity and speed of execution, a minor masterpiece.

"Thank you very much, Mr. Lowry, I will treasure it." Nathan would have it framed and hung in his room. " Would there be any chance of seeing your studio one day?"

"That would be fine, young man. I usually go out in the morning, so late afternoon would be best."

He gave Nathan his address – No.3, The Elms, Mottram-in-long-dendale.

When Nathan got home, he took great care in hanging the new

oil together with the two Lowrys he already had. He placed an arm-chair a few feet away and was quite happy to spend fifteen minutes just gazing at them, from one to the other then back again. Perfect tranquillity. It reflected life in his newly adopted town as seen through the eyes of his favourite artist, whom he thought the greatest ever.

CHAPTER 22

"I'm leaving. That's final." Nathan announced with as much authority as he could muster. He had been nagging his parents for some time to let him 'out,' as he put it. He had stuck it out at school, as he had promised he would, until he took his school certificate at sixteen. They had agreed to compromise and review the situation after the exams. He was not expecting brilliant results, maybe a few passes and a distinction in German, the one subject in which he excelled. They had these conversations at regular intervals. His parents were hoping to see him graduate sixth form then go to university.

Ilse tried again, "But you have settled in at school so nicely now, wouldn't it be sensible for you to go on?"

"Mother, we agreed that I could leave after the exams, if I wanted to and I do, I do, I really do," he half-shouted vehemently.

"Well darling, we just want what's best for you and a good education is so important, whatever career you're going in for."

"I detest school. I hate every minute I'm there and I insist – I do not want to go back, ever again."

"Alright, so you finish. Then what?"

"Just give me some space. Something will turn up."

Ilse sighed deeply. All the love she had given her only child and there was very little to show for it. They had built up a wonderful business but the conversation always came to an abrupt end when she pointed out that he had a superb opportunity to become a company director at an early age, and ultimately, take control. She knew what course the conversation would take, but tried yet again, "I'm spending three days in London next week. We're putting on a special show for a group of buyers from Marshall & Snelgrove."

"Mother, please don't go on…. Anyway, I've got choir practice every night next week, which I don't want to miss."

"It would be such fun to have you come with me. We could go to a show and have a really good time."

"Please don't go on and on."

But she did, "We've got two lovely models in the showroom. Cindy's your age. I'm sure she would love to meet you."

"Look Mother, for the last time," emphatically, "NO, NO, NO. I do not want to go into women's fashion. I DO NOT want to go into the family business, I do not like ladies clothing and I can't think of anything I would hate more."

And with that, he stormed out of the room, slamming the door behind him, taking refuge in his flat.

Whenever Nathan had an emotional upset, he would sit in his chair and stare into space, contemplating his Lowrys. Below, his mother was playing one of his favourite Beethoven sonatas, *No. 12, Opus 26*. He went downstairs and put his arms around her, "I'm sorry, Mother, I'm sorry."

He sat on the settee, listening to the sonata to the end. She played it beautifully.

When Arthur came into the room, he spoke seriously to his son,

"Now tell me something, Nathan. Why do you think we work round the clock sometimes seven days a week?"

"I suppose..." Nathan gave the question some thought before answering, "...that you work for the pleasure of seeing the company grow and flourish and to bring in enough money to live in luxury."

"True," he said, "but there is more to it than that. We are working to establish a company, which will pass on from one generation to the next. A company that will be there for as long as women buy the sort of clothes we make. We will survive the war. Generations will come and go, but Grunfelds, now the seeds are sown, must grow into a magnificent flower that will stay forever. Can you not understand, my dear son, that you are the link to the future? If you break that link, there will be no one to carry on the good work. It will be the end of the line. And that, Nathan, is why we put our heart and soul into the business that we love so much.... and hope that one day you will ensure our future."

"So I have a responsibility to the next generation that does not yet exist." Nathan replied, "Will it not be a hard task to ensure that

88

they share your interest in the company? Look at the difficulty you've had with me. Am I not likely to have the same problem with my children? Who can say what will be?"

"I agree, but we have to take one generation at a time."

Nathan sighed heavily and fell silent. Then Arthur sighed too. For it seemed that Nathan would not budge on this vital matter.

Nathan's voice broke. Now he was a tenor with a strident voice. He could sight read well and sing with perfect pitch. So polished a performer had he become that, in addition to the school choir, he joined the Hallé chorus, for which he had passed an audition with flying colours. Their resident conductor, John Barbirolli, was committed to using the full chorus for five concerts a year, the latest project being the Verdi Requiem, due to be performed in ten days. Chorus master Roger Wagner (no connection to the great Richard) had noticed the talent of his new young tenor and in mid 'sanctus', tapped his baton to signal a 'stop.'

"The timing is wrong, the tenors fluffed their entrance and the intonations are not correct." He looked at the score and said, "Nathan, would you mind giving us your interpretation?"

Nathan blushed to the roots of his hair, but understanding perfectly what Roger meant, gave a perfect pitch performance of the passage with the correct intonations.

Roger, applauding with his baton said, "Excellent. Now can we all do it like that?" And they did, to the delight of the chorus master.

It was not the first time he had noticed her. A pretty girl in the third row of the trebles. Shoulder length brown hair that flicked up at the ends, held by an Alice-band. An open friendly face. When she smiled she revealed glistening white teeth, perfectly placed. She was the youngest treble in the chorus and certainly the prettiest. Nathan, for all his shyness, had given her a generous appraisal, out of the corner of his eye as they sang in harmony.

Had he imagined that half way through 'Agnus Dei', she had smiled at him? He had looked away immediately, embarrassed. Now, as the chorus convened, his first, maybe subconscious act was to scan the treble benches to see if she was in her usual place. He watched her every move, until she accidentally looked in his direction.... causing Nathan to instantly look away.

After his solo, they somehow managed to file out simultaneously so that they were standing side by side.

She said, "You sang your solo beautifully."

He wanted to run away. "Oh well, I've sung it before," he lied nonchalantly, "so I knew how it went."

"Even so, you were very good."

She looked prettier up close. What on earth could he say next? Names perhaps. "My name is Nathan Grunfeld," he said.

"I know," she smiled, " I'm Helen Catchpole."

They shook hands. He was conscious that his palm was perspiring.

The next time they met, it was to rehearse the '*Te Deum*', the emotional and passionate conclusion of the Requiem. As they sang their parts, their eyes met on numerous occasions and they both smiled. The ice had been broken. Nathan had a game plan. He was going to pluck up courage after rehearsal to ask her if she would like to have a coffee.

"Well, I don't drink coffee," she laughed, "but if you were to suggest a milkshake, I might well say yes."

They both laughed when the waitress at the teashop they selected had never heard of a milkshake, let alone served one.

"What do you do?" Helen asked him.

"Nothing much, yet. I'm just finishing school. You?"

"I'm studying fashion design."

"Sounds good. You should meet my parents. They're in fashion."

"I'd like that."

As they talked about their respective families, hobbies and aspirations, the conversation began to flow quite freely. Helen was the daughter of a dentist, practising in Manchester, whose clientele included the rich and famous. Rich they had to be to meet his bills, which were high, famous, because he had the reputation of creating a winning smile. There was no better advertisement for his skills than Helen, who at the tender age of ten, was one of the first children to be seen in braces. Now her smile was bewitching and when Nathan made her laugh, which he did, mainly by telling jokes against himself, he was rewarded with a broad and beautiful smile.

Helen was three years older than Nathan, and as she revealed early in the evening, already the veteran of several relationships.

Whether these were ongoing, she did not disclose.

The time passed by so pleasantly, they hadn't noticed that all the tables had been cleared and that their 'friendly' waitress was standing over them holding a broom, "Excuse me Sir, Madam, but we're waiting to close."

At Helen's suggestion, they made a date to see the latest Deanna Durban film, '*Spring Parade*', at the Odeon in three days time. He wore a suit for the occasion, with white shirt and navy tie. He used his father's after-shave, just in case there might be close contact as he hoped. He looked handsome, but hopelessly innocent and immature.

Arthur drove him to the cinema, "So who is this cradle-snatcher you're seeing?" he teased.

Nathan told him the story of their meeting.

Arthur thought it amazing that he should have met her in exactly the same circumstances as he had met Ilse. And what a wonderful match that had been. It crossed his mind, that with his son on the brink of his first relationship, it was very remiss of him never to have sat down and introduced him to the facts of Life, man to man. There just had not been the time. Nathan had grown up so quickly. He just said, "Be careful!" Arthur did not give much thought to the fact that Helen was not Jewish. So what?

Since seeing her last, Nathan had spent two sleepless, anguishing nights under her spell, thinking of crazy things to do and say, which in the light of day, he dismissed immediately. They reached the Odeon and there she was in the foyer, looking quite stunning. Arthur caught a glimpse of her, "Wow. Not bad for your first date. If you need any help, just give me a call."

The evening was a great success. They held hands in the back row of the one and nine penny stalls and, even before the Wurlitzer organ had appeared from below, he had put his arm around her shoulder. She showed no sign of rejecting his attentions. He couldn't remember too much about the film, but she said it was good and he believed her. He had been more preoccupied with who was sitting beside him and his next move.

Walking home, the conversation touched on sexual matters. Nathan blushed visibly. He did not admit to being a virgin, but the naiveté in his questioning made it fairly obvious.

"When do you decide whether to have an affair or not," he asked coyly.

The voice of experience, "You don't decide, it just happens."

"And if you don't want it to happen?"

"I wouldn't be with that person in the first place."

Encouraged, Nathan smiled nervously, "Does that mean you might do it with me?" As soon as he said it, he wished he hadn't. It was like bringing your Queen out too early in a game of chess. But he need not have worried.

"With a voice like yours, anything could happen," she said with a twinkle in her eye.

By now, Nathan was on a high. He was intoxicated with her beauty, sexuality and smile. He would have liked to hold her in his arms and kiss her, but was nervous that any such move might be rejected.

As he said 'goodnight', he risked a peck on her cheek. She responded with a passionate kiss full on the lips. It was the most exciting moment of his life.

"I think I have fallen in love with you," he said shakily and prematurely.

She kissed him again, more lingeringly this time, then said seductively, "There's a lot more to come."

Whenever the Hallé Orchestra and Chorus conducted by Sir John Barbirolli performed in Manchester, it was a big occasion and a sell out. Arthur and Ilse were there, as were Helen's parents, not only in support of their offspring, but also for the major musical experience that lay ahead.

Verdi had composed the *Requiem* out of deep mourning and despair at the death of his friend, the great Italian Poet and Novelist Allessandro Manzetti, who died in 1873. Verdi had idolised him and the *Requiem* reflected the passion of his feelings. It was a deeply felt piece and listening to it, let alone performing it, was an enduring and emotionally draining experience.

However, that night, Nathan and Helen seemed oblivious to its gravity, keeping eye contact throughout much of their performance. The beauty of the *Requiem* seemed to sharpen their senses, heighten their anticipation for the inevitable meeting that would take place later.

Nathan had separate access to his flat upstairs, which he could use without going through the house. It was there, that the pent-up emotion of the evening was to find its fulfilment. The sight of Helen undressed sent Nathan into a frenzy. He showered her with a torrent of kisses.

At the height of his passion, Helen reached for her bag. She said softly, without emotion, "You'd better wear one of these things."

But it was too late. The excitement had been too much for a first timer.

CHAPTER 23

It was extraordinary that Nathan's first sexual experience should have changed his personality. From a gauche, introvert teenager, who never said much, he had become an eloquent, confident young man who could talk to anyone about anything. He would tell jokes, mimic Hitler, with forefinger over upper lip for moustache and, pushing hair over his forehead, he would launch into a tirade of Hitler jargon. His parody was funny and his audience, by laughing heartily, would encourage him to further excesses. He was at his best when Helen was with him, and having become as flamboyant as she, it was like a double act bouncing 'funnies' from one off the other. Acquaintances who might have sought to avoid him, now went out of their way to talk to him, since it might, they thought, lead to an introduction to the outstanding girl he had on his arm. While she was around, he was the centre of attraction.

On one occasion, they attended an engagement party and Nathan was asked, unexpectedly, to say a few words. He ad-libbed with such wit, drew such laughter and applause from all assembled, that Helen rushed over and kissed him passionately, "My reward," he said with outstretched arms to more applause.

Of course, there were more visits to the first floor and it was after one of these that Ilse, who had heard the sound of their love-making quite distinctly through the ceiling, asked, "About time you introduced us isn't it?"

"Sure," he said, "I'll bring her round."

Naturally, they had to leave the flat by the street entrance and ring the front door bell.

"How nice to meet you at last," Ilse greeted them, "Nathan never stops talking about you. And he's right. All those nice things he says about you..."

They had a pleasant conversation over tea and biscuits, during which Helen told of her fashion design studies and was delighted to accept an invitation to look over the factory.

"You'll find it very interesting," said Ilse and, with a smile, "Perhaps you could bring my son with you. He hasn't been near the place for over a year."

When they arrived at the factory the following day, Ilse sent her apologies. She was tied up for the moment and would join them later. Meanwhile Lotzie Papp would show them around.

The machine park was now working at full capacity. Twenty-five circular and four flat machines need a lot of looking after and clatter noisily as they knit, making conversation difficult. Lotzi felt the need to explain how each machine was fed with yarn spools of different colours, through a ring of needles, then knitting wheels to formulate the required design. As the giant machines turned around, the fabric would appear as though by magic, in its basin. He did not need to be too explicit, since Helen's course had covered knitting plant and she was happy to show off her knowledge. She wandered from machine to machine, studying the fabric each one produced.

Nathan had never before taken much interest in how the machines worked, but Helen's excitement stimulated his pride in the family business.

"Impressed?"

"And how," she replied, "but some of the designs could be so much more fashionable and modern if the colours were different."

Lotzi was reluctant to agree, but he had often had discussions with Ilse on how to rejuvenate a design by changing the colour concept.

"Take this design for example. Lotzi, could you give me a little cutting? It's a lovely design, but how dull it is using grey as the basic colour. If this were ecru with a touch of fuchsia, it would be a young girls design instead of an old woman's."

Lotzi nodded, "Shall we change the colours around that way and see how it looks?"

"Great," she said enthusiastically.

He showed his dexterity in replacing the grey colour spools with ecru and fuchsia, threaded the yarn through he needles, pressed the start button and within a few moments, the machine produced the new colour.

Nathan was the first to speak, "God. What a difference. Chalk and cheese."

But Helen was not done, "Can we knit some trimmings on the flat machine to match? I'd like to see a needle-out tweedy braid using the same colours on an ecru base about one inch wide."

Lotzi knew exactly what she meant. He changed the spools on the flat machine and, within a short time, had produced a yard of the required braid.

"Fantastic," Helen said, "you're so clever." She then held the fabric, edging it with the braid. A blind person could have seen what a beautiful blend it was and how vibrant the colours now looked. Next she asked Lotzi for pen and paper. Within minutes, she had produced a skilful working drawing of the design she envisaged, ready for the sample room.

Lotzi said, "Best design I've seen in years."

At this moment, Ilse arrived, apologising profusely for being late. Lotzi did not have to explain. The fabric, sketch and braid in his hand were self-explanatory. She took it all in within a moment, then turning to Lotzi, she said in a voice loud enough to be heard above the machine clatter, "I would ask you Lotzi kindly not to change designs and colours without authorisation," and even more icily, "We have lost valuable production time. Never do that again."

Nathan interrupted, "Sorry, Mother, it's all my fault. I asked Helen to do a design and look what she came up with. Lotzi thinks its great and so do I. Look, what a lovely sketch."

Ilse looked at it disdainfully, "I am sure she designs very well, but we supply a middle-of-the-road clientele, who do not take kindly to any innovations."

Nathan felt that, by reprimanding Lotzi so publicly, his mother had been very offensive towards their guest. He leapt to defend Helen, who now looked most embarrassed, "Lotzi thinks it's the best design he's seen for a long time."

"Really."

"So why not consider the sketch and the new colour-way?"

"Because I decide what design we make. I do the sales and I know exactly what our clients require." With that, she turned to leave them, but not before she had snatched from Lotzi's hand, the sketch, fabric and braid.

On the return journey, Helen could not stop apologizing for the trouble she had caused. How could she have been so impertinent? She felt terrible. She must write to Ilse at once and apologize, and to Lotzi as well. It was the biggest 'faux pas' in her life.

Nathan comforted her, "Not at all. It's obvious. There is a massive opportunity to modernize the design and colour blending. And you showed what could be done. You meant no harm. You weren't going to take over the company. You're not a threat. It was all so innocent, not worth a whole great scene."

"I must say," said Helen, "I would love to be let loose with those machines. Lotzi could make them talk and with my design ideas, we could really revolutionise the place."

Nathan kissed her and said, "You have shown how talented you are."

"Now, listen to me, Nathan," she said, with the air of someone about to give a lecture, "I have known you now for six months. During that time, you have been drifting around and haven't done a stroke of work." She repeated, "Not a stroke. Nor have you made any attempt to get a job or choose a career. Your parents have a brilliant business, with massive potential. You are the son and heir and you take no interest in it whatsoever. I can't believe it. They must be longing for you to be involved, even if you only sweep up."

"Yes, I'd be good at that," he said, trying to make light of her strong language.

But she had more to say, "I will lose my respect for you totally if you don't roll up your sleeves and learn the business from A to Z."

Helen's visit had opened his eyes to the opportunity he had, and how foolish he had been to turn his back on his parents' brilliant enterprise. He was not prepared to say so at once, but had certainly taken her message to heart.

"And once you're there," she continued, "you can appoint me as your designer."

That very evening, when he joined his parents for dinner, he broached the subject by no easy route, "Helen wants to write to you and apologise for the intrusion."

"That won't be necessary," Ilse replied, obviously still smarting from the assault on her territory, "I quite understand how a younger person might try to introduce new ideas, but that was not the way to do it."

"She didn't mean to insult you. She was just expressing herself. She thought it was a brilliant set-up." He paused for effect. He knew his next sentence would make an impact. "I must say, it was quite an eye-opener for me as well. Perhaps it is time I got involved."

His parents exchanged a look, trying to conceal their delight. This was a sentiment they thought that they would never hear.

Ilse said, "That's wonderful news, darling. We'll teach you everything and make you a Director at once."

Arthur said, "I would go happy to my grave, if I knew I had secured the business for at least the next generation."

Nathan was moved. He walked over to his father and embraced him. "Father, you are a long way from being in your grave. And yes, I promise you faithfully that the business will be secure for the next generation, at the very least."

Ilse said, "Lets drink a toast to the future Managing Director."

Nathan had made a commitment and was not one to go back on his word. He wondered whether his parents realised why this change of heart had come about so suddenly. He came to the point, "With all this talk about future generations, I have found someone with whom I hope to share my life …. And perhaps be blessed with children."

"Nathan, you're only seventeen. Boys of your age don't talk of marriage and children," Ilse said quickly.

"But Mother, don't you see how in love we are? How she's changed my life. I would be nothing without her."

"You can be good friends, yes, and for a long time. But at seventeen you should not have these crazy ideas."

"Mother, I love her. She makes me happy and she loves me. How else can it end but in marriage and children? We are inseparable, totally."

Ilse cringed at the prospect of marriage, "She's not even Jewish,"

"She can convert. Lots of people do. She'll be happy to do it. Anyway, she's a very talented designer as we saw this morning. If I join the business, which I hope to do Monday morning, I would like her to join the company as your assistant, Mother, and become a junior designer. If that could happen, I'd be so happy."

Ilse greeted this bombshell with a stunned silence. Finally

bristling, "I do not think that would be a very good idea."

"But why, Mother? We could be a brilliant team, the four of us."

"I do not think that your father and I are quite ready to retire yet. And I, for one do not relish the idea of a stranger in the company holding high office."

"High office?" he echoed. "Hardly. I did say junior and your assistant."

"And for how long?" she asked cynically.

Nathan played his trump card, "I am sorry to have to say that if there can be no place for as talented a designer as Helen in the company, with whom I happen to be in love, then there can be no place for me either."

Arthur, with the Wisdom of Solomon, said, "I would like to make a proposal with which I hope all parties can agree. Nathan will join the business on Monday morning. It will be a pleasure to have you with us, my son. We will teach you everything we know. If in two years time, you still feel the same way about Helen as you do now, I am sure that your Mother will then agree for her to join as a junior designer."

They both agreed to Arthur's proposal.

But the next morning, Ilse looked for Helen's sketch amongst her papers and tore it into small pieces.

CHAPTER 24

Relations were terse for a while between Mother and son. Ilse found it difficult to conceal her dislike of Nathan's girlfriend, seeing her as an intruder in their lives and a threat to the great love that they had for one another.

Although the subject was never raised again, it was always on her mind, and whenever she detected Nathan was not alone in the flat upstairs, she was distressed to think of her beloved son intimate with the woman she regarded as her rival for his affections. On one occasion, when she heard them giggling happily upstairs, Ilse could control her emotions no longer and telephoned her son in the flat, requesting less noise.

Arthur knew exactly what was going on in Ilse's mind, "Let the young people enjoy themselves," he said.

"She's no better than a common tart, coming to our house and carrying on with our son the way she does. Under our very roof; its disgusting."

"Ilse, please don't be too possessive of him. He's enjoying his first love affair. Let him be happy. He's doing well in the business. I think it is only because of her influence that he's joined us."

"Yes, with only one thing in mind, to get herself a job. My job." Then she muttered darkly, "Mark my words, Arthur, that girl's after more than Nathan. She won't be happy till the sign over the factory reads: Grunfeld & Catchpole..."

Soon their attention turned to more important matters – Hitler's Blitzkreig had annihilated his Eastern neighbours. Now his might was pointed westwards. The imminent collapse of the Maginot line, France's 'impenetrable' defence structure, would inevitably lead France into capitulation, and it would not be long before Hitler's image, strutting arrogantly down the Champs Elysees, would be flashed around the world. It had become public knowledge that as they swept through one country after another, the Jews were rounded up, locked into airless cattle trucks before being shunted to the concentration camps.

After France, it would be England, with only twenty miles of channel separating Hitler's crack divisions and the White cliffs of Dover. Air Chief Marshall Dowding, much to the disgust of the now wilting French regime, had ordered his Spitfire squadrons in France to return home, in readiness for the Battle of Britain. Defence at home was now a greater priority than trying to stem the tide in France.

It was not surprising then, that the Grunfelds, wanting to err on the side of caution, seriously contemplated whether they should pack up and leave, to put some distance between themselves and the Nazi's possible arrival in England. If that ever happened, they, as German fugitives, would be first on the Gestapo hit list.

But where to go? There was no obvious choice. They decided to wait and see. Winston Churchill had, meanwhile, entered the arena and his tough, rallying speeches gave them hope and the confidence to stay put, praying that Mr. Churchill would deliver his promises – the ultimate destruction of the Nazi regime.

Surprisingly, in these critical times, business continue to flourish. The team, now strengthened by Nathan's participation, worked well. Five of their number had been called up for military service.

Nathan, now nearly eighteen, was bracing himself for a similar fate. He was bemused by the way in which his mother and girlfriend reacted so differently to his oncoming enlistment. Ilse was scheming desperately to find an excuse. Could she claim that his ordeal in Germany had left him psychologically deranged? Or that his role at work was vital in helping to keep the company going? She even insisted on a doctor's appointment to establish whether flat feet, poor eyesight or any other ailment could be pushed forward, all to no avail.

Helen, on the other hand, had quite the reverse attitude, "Of course you must join up," she said, "I would lose respect for you if you didn't. I shall join up myself. The A.T.S. are looking for able-bodied women, and that I certainly am. This is the time for all of us to stand and be counted." She was patriotic to her fingertips and scoffed at Ilse's attempts to get him off. "Stupid woman," she muttered, for the first time voicing disapproval.

But Nathan was ready to serve his adopted country. Not because of Helen's encouragement, but simply because he wanted to be like everyone else. He loved his Manchester surroundings where he felt at home, and if the butcher, baker and postman went to fight the common enemy, then why shouldn't he? He also felt, more than most, such a violent hatred of the Nazi regime, that he cherished the thought of personal vendetta.

He did not have to wait long for his call-up papers, which arrived precisely one week before his eighteenth birthday. A buff envelope, 'On His Majesty's Service,' gave him seven days to report to his new unit, the Kings Regiment, at Catterick. Ilse was beside herself with grief as she drove him to Piccadilly Station with Arthur and Helen.

As they waited on the platform, Helen said, "I'm so proud of you, going to fight for your country."

Ilse sniped at her, "You are a bad influence on him. You have no idea what he went through in Germany. He should be allowed to stay home, to look after his business."

It was open warfare between them. But they were nonetheless united in grief as the train steamed away and they stayed waving, until, looking out of the window, he finally disappeared from sight.

Ilse could have saved her tears. When Nathan revealed at his first interview that he was bilingual, he was immediately seconded to the Intelligence Corps. He was offered a commission without attending the Officer Cadet Training Unit. He underwent an intensive training course, at the end of which he emerged with fluent shorthand in both English and German, and the ability to translate freely from one language to the other.

His job was to monitor German war reports, listen in to the speeches and prepare an English translation for his commanding officer, who would then report to Whitehall. He became so proficient, that he could even follow Hitler's rapid delivery and record every word into perfect translated English. As he said to his CO, "You take one of his speeches, Sir, and you have the lot. He says the same thing every time. Just varies the raving and ranting."

After a while, he became senior translator and promoted to Captain. When he arrived home for a forty-eight hour leave and revealed three pips on his shoulder, Arthur and Ilse could hardly contain their pride. Even Helen was impressed, "What on earth is the British Army doing with its Officers? Captains must be two a penny." She, meanwhile, had become a private in the A.T.S., and looked enormously attractive in uniform. They would spend quite a lot of his leave on the first floor flat to rekindle their love affair.

Forty-eight hour passes came every eight weeks, for which he always found his way home. The joy at seeing his parents was surpassed only by the wonderful days and nights he spent with Helen in the privacy of his little flat.

After one such visit, Ilse had dental problems. Her dentist felt it necessary to extract two of her teeth. She didn't take kindly to any form of surgery and sought a second opinion. A good opportunity she thought, to consult Mr. Catchpole, Helen's father, who offered to crown her teeth to save their extraction.

No one can conjecture what dialogue passed between them. Maybe it was coincidence. But the fact remains that some two weeks later Nathan received a letter from Helen:

Nathan, my darling,
This will be the hardest letter I have ever written. Please blame the war as much as me. These are terrible times and it is impossible to make rational decisions. Excuse the smudge... my hand is shaking as I write. I tried... but I could not. The fact is... that I have agreed to marry someone I love with all my heart. That does not mean that I do not love you too, because I do. Truly. But Mike Baker and I have a lot in common. He is three years older than I am and because his parents were killed in the Blitz, he needs me now badly. I am his only family. Because he is flying Spitfires, where anything can happen, he wants to get married quickly.

I feel I owe him a positive answer. I would have given it to him sooner, were it not for my love for you. You are still so young and have time to find so many other girls – particularly now that you are a Captain. We have had a great time together and I will always have a place in my heart for you. I know that you will be just as heart-broken receiving this letter as I am writing it. Please don't try to ring or write. It will only make things worse.

All my love, my sweetheart, I will always love you, no matter what.
Helen.

Nathan read the letter over and over again. He was ashen. After its devastating contents had sunk in, he went back to his work. It was not until the evening that he threw himself on his bed and sobbed, as he had never done before.

A PACT

CHAPTER 25

I felt inclined to join in his grief. Even as he related the story several years later, tears welled in Nathan's eyes. He pulled out a handkerchief, "I loved that girl," he said after a few moments, "she was my life, my soul. We were made for each other."

I tried to console him, "But your parents – would they ever have accepted her?"

"They could see she made me happy. What more could they wish for their son?" he sighed, "You can only expect to love so deeply once in a lifetime; and that was it. I shall never love like that again."

I was reminded of my own passion for Gisela. It occurred to me that Nathan and I had moved forward on such parallel lines, until destiny brought us together at Nüremburg.

He said, "You know, Thomas, I really want you to write my story now I've told you so much. It's the only way Helen will ever know how much she meant to me. You will you do it, won't you? Will you promise?"

I picked up the sheaf of papers on which I had taken notes. "It's all here," I said, "all I need is peace of mind and time."

We were sitting in the Officers' Mess on the same lounger chairs that we had occupied every day for the last two weeks. Our 'office desk' was a round mahogany table, now littered with coffee cups and remains of the day's pipes.

I beckoned the raven-haired waitress to our table to order more coffee and biscuits – our third round in as many hours. I noticed her shapely legs clad in nylons, a clear indication that she was dating a G.I. When she returned with two cups of steaming Nescafé, I asked her name. She replied with a smile, "Waltraute. My friends call me Traute."

I moved forward in my chair and said in German, "It's very nice to meet you, Traute. Tell me, where do the beautiful girls like you get to in the evening?"

She blushed to the roots of her hair. I judged her to be no more than seventeen years old. She replied, "There are three or four night spots in town. Good music and much fun."

"And which of these would you think most suitable for my friend and I?"

This sent her off into a fit of giggles. Perhaps she concluded that we were not suited to such an ambiance at all. After a moment, she recovered enough to say, "I would say that 'Der Heisse Vogel' is the best for gentlemen like you."

"And if we go tonight, will you be there?"

"Maybe. It depends on my boyfriend." With that, she considered the joke as over and walked away.

I passed Nathan the biscuits. He dunked them in his Nescafé as he always did. He smiled at me wryly, "Cradle snatcher," he mumbled, his mouth full of biscuit.

"Maybe," I replied evenly, "but she's old enough for someone else." Then I added casually, "fancy going for a look?"

The idea seemed to cheer him up, "OK, I get the hint. Enough talking. Let's get screwing."

CHAPTER 26

In those early post-war days, the nicest German girls of good families could be 'acquired' for a tin of Nescafé, such was the poverty and famine level of the population. G.I.s were favoured, but two good-looking German-speaking Englishmen had plenty to offer and the language asset gave them a head start over their American rivals.

The local entrepreneurs had been quick to realise that G.I.s were going to need entertainment and had converted the former 'Gasthof' into a nightclub, christened 'Der Heisse Vogel' – The Hot Bird. The band played non-stop Glen Miller and the club was soon doing a roaring trade.

At weekends, the place was packed with army personnel and attractive girls, eager to be hospitable. If the bar and dancing area was a money-spinner, the rooms above were a goldmine. The owners had vacated their living accommodation to provide twelve self-contained rooms, which could be hired by the hour or night.

We saw Waltraute the moment we walked in. She was giggling with a group of girls, whilst canoodling with her GI boyfriend, a Master Sergeant in the Air Force. She introduced us to two of the girls standing with her unescorted and we bought them drinks. Heidi and Erica seemed nice girls with no less sex appeal than Waltraute. Having met us and established that we spoke their language, they were not going to let us go. There was a delicate moment, when we made them aware that they had landed a couple of 'Jewish guys'. Heidi's comments spoke volumes:

"After all the propaganda, it's hard to believe. You're so normal, just like all the other boys."

Nathan and I had our reservations. We were befriending two girls, whose fathers, uncles, brothers might well have been Gestapo or SS. It was not easy at the outset, but the flesh is weak, and before we had given the conflict in our minds a second thought, we had a few dances with them, then offered to take them to the 'Services Club', which they accepted with relish.

They ate with more enthusiasm than the food deserved. They told us that they could hardly survive on the meagre rations, which had decreased alarmingly over the last year. No food could be bought in the shops and a Black Market trade was rampant, which only the wealthy could afford. We produced a box of chocolate bars, which they tore open and consumed hungrily, stuffing the rest into their bags.

At first I was reluctant to admit to a common language with the German girls, lest I be classified as one of them. But as the evening developed, I was enjoying the German conversation and happy to be bilingual, since the girls' English seemed to consist of only one phrase, which they threw into the conversation frequently – 'I love you.' Their body language was very sexual and it was obvious that the girls were seeking a relationship.

Nathan's girl, Erica, was half a head taller than he was and as we left, he stood on tiptoe, looked up into her eyes with some difficulty, and said, "Don't you worry darling, I'm king-size in other areas"

The girls roared with laughter. We agreed to meet again at the 'Heisse Vogel', three days later and promised them another meal and more chocolate.

On this, our second date, we were invited to take advantage of the facilities upstairs. Once tried, never repeated. The beds were stained and the rooms filthy. Used condoms and empty packets were everywhere. Luckily, both girls had bought clean towels with them. I winked at Nathan and said, "They've done it before."

There were only two communal toilets to go round and a queue of both sexes, scantily clad and looking sheepish, was a little embarrassing. Sordid it may have been, but it gave me the opportunity of getting to know Heidi intimately. Her body was slender, flat-chested and legs too thin. I could probably help her gain weight with the food that was available to us. She had a pretty face though, showing attractive dimples as she smiled and short blonde hair permed into waves in the style of the day. She was a 'fun' girl, very keen on tennis and swimming, in which we were to indulge later.

The two girls were to become our source of relaxation and we remained friends throughout the trial and after. Whenever we entertained them, food was still their overriding interest and we took them to the best places available to Service personnel.

As we got to know them better, the topics of conversation moved beyond 'small talk.' Nathan got onto the subject of the Renoir paintings his family owned, until stolen by the Nazis on orders believed to have emanated from Hermann Göring.

Heidi said at once, "Surely you will get them back now the war is over."

Nathan replied, "First you have to find them."

"Well," Heidi persisted, "if Göring had anything to do with it, and he is now in a cell at Nüremburg, surely you can walk in there and demand their return or at least an explanation of where they are."

There was no immediate reaction from either of us. We were dumfounded at the simplicity of her idea. Nathan and I exchanged glances in silence.

He spoke first. His face lit up, "It's a fantastic idea. We should have done that ages ago." He embraced Heidi, "You are so clever to think of the obvious."

I said, "Amazing isn't it. We have to go out with a German girl, who tells us what we should have done the moment Göring was moved in."

We kissed both girls in a mood of euphoria, excited by the prospect of confronting the former Reichsmarshall. After some thought, Nathan said, "A wonderful idea in theory, but how do we put it into practice? We can't just knock on the door and march in. It has to be an official visit."

I had an idea. The previous day I had spoken with a Scottish Officer, who I thought might help. Major Alistair McNaughton was an aristocratic gentleman who was going from cell to cell discussing legal representation and indictments with each of the accused. I had met him in the cafeteria around midday the previous day, at which time it was his custom to take a break. Now I lay in wait for him, pretending to read a paper.

Not for long. He occupied his usual table at the usual time, taking tea and biscuits alone. I plucked up courage and went over to him. I needed to show considerable respect. He was a Major, and I, a mere 2nd Lieutenant. "Good morning Sir," I said tentatively, "Do you mind if I join you for a moment? I would very much appreciate your guidance on a personal matter."

"Of course," He was charm itself, "If I can help. Take a seat."

He shifted a few papers to make room for me and I launched into Nathan's problem.

The Major listened carefully and considered the matter. Finally he said, "A bit hard on the poor old chap, when he's fighting for his life."

Alistair McNaughton was known to be very fair and protective towards the prisoners, and as I later found out, a stickler for protocol.

I urged Nathan to try another avenue. Colonel 'Buster' Andrews was the American commandant in total charge of all the prisoners. He had landed the job for his known hatred of the Nazi regime. He was a tough, no-nonsense, strict disciplinarian, who nonetheless, had gained the respect of the prisoners. He regarded his job as being 'to keep the bums alive until the hangman released him from that responsibility.' He had no doubt in his mind of the guilt of 'the Goddam bloody lot'. What was more he was engaged in a one-to-one, ongoing psychological feud with Göring.

When Nathan approached him with his story, he was sympathetic and saw the opportunity for putting his quarry under further pressure. "Sure", he said, "I'm gonna see the guy at nine am tomorrow. Be my guest."

CHAPTER 27

"Face to face with the enemy," Nathan puzzled, "How the hell do I handle that? Do I talk English or German? Do I shake hands?"

"Just play it by ear." I tried to reassure him, "'Buster' will be speaking in English, so it would be disrespectful if you broke into German. Anyway, Göring's the underdog now. You have the initiative. Let him struggle with the language."

"I'd like him to know I'm Jewish. Could you lend me your Star of David?"

"I'm sure he'll work it out, but if you think it'll help..."

I undid the clasp and put it around his neck. It hung too low to be visible beneath his jacket and he asked me to shorten the chain, so that it could be seen.

Colonel Andrews suggested that Nathan should get his first impression of the man and his surroundings, by looking through the porthole, before they went in.

The former Reichsmarshall was pacing the length of his lair, no more than three paces, like a caged tiger. He held some papers in one hand and gesticulated with the other, as though rehearsing his response to the indictment. Most of the cell seemed to be taken up by the bunk bed so small that Nathan wondered how a big man could lie on it in any sort of comfort. Opposite, there was a primitive washbasin. The toilet could not be seen from the porthole, which gave a blind spot to the cell, of which Robert Ley, a prominent Nazi, had taken advantage to kill himself.

Colonel Andrews, sensitive to this risk, had installed a powerful spotlight beamed onto a mirror, as well as a twenty-four hour guard, to ensure that there were no further suicides.

The first thing that struck Nathan was his odd shape. Göring was short. He was around five foot six tall, but had the frame of what had obviously been a very large man with a substantial girth. Now

111

having lost massive weight, the fat folds hung about him like deflated balloons. While his face, once rounded, was now gaunt and heavily lined, his chin sagged well below his neck. His hair was unkempt, his chin stubbled. He was wearing baggy trousers that rested on his lower hip, revealing the mounds of floppy flesh that had once been a taut overfilled belly. Without belt or braces, his trousers were in constant danger of falling to his thighs and he hoisted them up several times as he continued his deliberations, unaware that he was being scrutinised. He wore a butcher's type vest, with three top buttons undone, to reveal a heavy growth of hair around his lower neck.

And this, thought Nathan, this was Hitler's number one man – the man once destined to take over on Hitler's suicide and lead the Third Reich out of the chaos of its own making. As the triple lock of the cell was opened, Nathan followed the Colonel Andrews into the cell.

"Good morning, Göring," said the Colonel. "Sleep OK?"

It was a statement. No answer was expected, but this was Göring, who never missed the opportunity for repartee.

"How can I sleep with that confounded light on all night?" he demanded, pointing his chubby finger at the light above the door. "And the bed is ridiculous. If you were even pretending to abide by the Geneva convention..."

The Colonel interrupted, "I have brought Captain Grunfeld to see you. He wants to ask you some questions."

Mercifully, no handshake was offered. Nathan was tempted to say 'How do you do,' or 'How are you keeping?' but before he could do so, Göring turned to Nathan and, addressing him in reasonable English, said, "You know Captain, this so called trial is a total farce. It is no more than victor's justice, pure and simple. Because the Americans won the war, they are the victors who now want to punish the losers. Wars have been fought for centuries. It is..."

Colonel Andrews interrupted him rudely in mid sentence, "Göring, will you please quit? The Captain has not got all day to listen to your claptrap and nor have I."

This was Nathan's cue to state his business. He fingered his 'Star of David' nervously to ensure it was not wasted on Göring, began

"Before the war, my parents lived in Berlin where they owned some Renoir paintings..."

Now, Göring smiled, revealing several gold teeth. Where before he had been sullen, now his voice was silky, "Ah, but I love the Impressionists. What a pleasure to meet a fellow collector."

"The paintings were stolen from them as they left the country. I am here on their behalf to ask you if you can tell me where they are now."

Nathan persevered, trying to be pleasant, "How many do you have?"

"It is not a question of how many I have," answered Göring, pompously, "It is a question of how beautiful they are. And these works of art belong to the German people."

"And how did this collection of paintings come into the ownership of the German people?"

With yet another broad smile, Göring said, "You know how it is. Museums acquire pictures from here, there and everywhere."

Nathan decided to cut the formality, "Look, those Renoirs were stolen from my family by the Nazis. Now the war is over, we want them back. I understand that your Karinhall is full of stolen works of art, collected from all over Europe. I want to know whether our pictures are on your walls."

This was delivered as a blunt statement of fact, with Göring taking it in, still smiling as though he was having a conversation about art, his favourite topic, "You are quite wrong, my friend. You think that these treasures were obtained illegally? Far from it. The Führer allocated a substantial budget to enrich the Reich with works of art for the people of Germany to enjoy and pass on from one generation to the next."

Exasperated, Nathan said, "Our pictures were taken from us illegally without payment. There was no budget involved."

"Look", said Göring in his most reasonable tone, "When this ridiculous trial is over, I will invite you to Karinhall as my guest to view my collection. If you recognise your pictures, which I doubt, I am sure we can come to some amicable arrangement."

Nathan was losing his composure. Through clenched teeth, he said, "I am not looking for 'an amicable arrangement.' All I am trying to establish is where the pictures are now." He tried again,

113

"Do you have any Renoirs in your collection?"

"Ah yes," Göring was smiling at the memory, "I have quite a few…"

"And if I gave you the name of one of our pictures, would you admit that you had it?"

"My dear, Captain," he said grandly, "I do not know my pictures by name. Only by their beauty."

Nathan was on to his final fling, "One of our pictures is called, *La Baigneuse*. It shows a beautiful woman preparing to swim."

For a fraction of a second, a look of recognition flitted across Göring's face that told all. They both knew it. The game was up. He recovered quickly, to say, "Maybe I have seen it. Maybe I have not. There are so many Renoirs in our museums." He smiled again but was not going to say any more.

Nathan felt that the meeting had been worthwhile, and was sure that *La Baigneuse*, at least, if not the others, would be found in the palace of this odious man.

As Nathan left the cell, Göring called after him, "Don't forget my invitation, Captain. After the trial I hope to see you at my home."

Nathan did not answer. He was relieved to hear the cell door close behind him and the clank of the triple locks being securely bolted.

CHAPTER 28

Flanked by a contingent of armed Military Police, the twenty-two prisoners were finally ushered into the dock.

They were whispering amongst themselves, even joking as they filed into their allotted places. I saw no heads bowed in abject apology. Indeed, their body language was carefree, light-hearted as though the outing had no purpose other than for them to chat with their mates. I could detect only defiance in their attitude, no feelings of guilt for the heinous crimes of which they stood accused.

A feeling of disgust and hatred came over me as I cast my eye along the line of these now pathetic men, deprived of their power and status, wearing shabby prison made suits or tatty lived-in uniforms without insignia or rank.

When the prosecution got under way, it soon became clear that Göring led the pack. He revelled in the star role he had assumed and enjoyed baiting the American prosecutor, Robert Jackson, to the great amusement of his fellow prisoners. At one stage, they applauded until called to order by the presiding judge, Francis Biddle.

Encouraged by some early successes, Göring attempted to take centre stage and address the jury to develop his by now familiar theories until firmly put down by the judge, "Would you please be seated, Mr. Göring? This is a court of law and we cannot allow you to make ad hoc speeches when it suits you. You will have your opportunity to state your case under cross-examination."

He replied under his breath, "Ah, but by then I will have forgotten," to more titters from the rest of the gang.

But the role of court jester did him no favours in the long run. The tables were well and truly turned on him when the English prosecutor, Sir David Maxwell-Fyfe, sought justice for the RAF officers who had mass-escaped from Luft Stalag camp and who, on recapture, had been shot dead in cold blood by the Gestapo. It was a moment of high drama when he produced a document and asked the usher to pass it to the accused.

"Have you seen this document before?" he asked.

Göring replied, "Thousands of orders and documents have gone through my office. When you are Reichsmarshall and engaged in warfare, there is a constant stream of papers..."

The judge intervened, "You have been asked a simple question by Sir David, requiring a simple reply. Have you or have you not seen the document in question?"

"It is possible, I cannot say for sure. I may have seen it, but not read it."

Maxwell-Fyfe pressed home his advantage, "This paper is an order to shoot in cold blood those POWs who had the misfortune to be recaptured," and then turning squarely to face the accused, "Would you be kind enough to inform the court whose signature it is at the foot of that treacherous order?"

An onlooker in the visitors' gallery whispered, "Get out of that one, Hermann."

But for once, he had been silenced.

A thirty-minute film was projected, showing the nightmare of Belsen concentration camp and the horrors to which those poor souls had been subjected. The few survivors were represented by Joseph Schulman who spoke movingly about the mental and physical torture the inmates had suffered, and how he was able to survive only by virtue of his previous employment – that of grave-digger. The film sealed the fate of those accused that were involved with the death camps.

The military men were not able to escape the ultimate penalty by claiming they were 'obeying orders.' There was surprise that three men had achieved acquittal and the Russians issued a statement disassociating their country from this decision, which they had done everything in their power to veto.

Albert Speer got off with twenty years, maybe because of his abject apology and remorse. "I was misled," he claimed.

But his deputy, Fritz Sauckel, had no such luck and was sentenced to hang for his activity with slave labour. The final score was: twelve to hang, three for life imprisonment, four for ten to

116

twenty years imprisonment.

When Nathan translated Göring's verdict, "Tod durch den Strang," he was inwardly rejoicing and speaking revenge for his family and six million Jews who perished in the holocaust.

But Hermann had the last laugh after all. Ten hours before his execution was due to take place he managed to kill himself with cyanide.

CHAPTER 29

As Ilse and Arthur, flanked by Nathan and the curator, walked across the vast expanse of marble floor, towards the pictures on the far wall, Ilse let out a gasp and clutched Arthur's arm. Pencil rays of light with dancing dust suspended in them, filtered through the long, leaded casement windows, played on the surface of the Renoirs, making them even more luminous than she remembered them to be.

Nathan had brought his parents back to Germany to inspect the paintings and now they stood, dwarfed by the high ceilings of the gallery of Karinhall, the grand country estate house that had once belonged to Hermann Göring.

"Our paintings," said Ilse, tremulously, "And now, at last, we shall have them back."

But it was not to be so simple.

As the curator explained, there was a claims procedure and the onus of proof of ownership was on the claimant.

"But, of course we can prove it," said Arthur, "Why, for years, those paintings hung in our house. Everyone we knew saw them. Our neighbours. They will vouch that the paintings are ours..."

But Ilse's brow furrowed. Many of their erstwhile neighbours were dead, or scattered to the four winds – some in the United States, others in Palestine.

"We'll track our neighbours down," said Arthur, "get depositions from them..."

"I'm afraid that wouldn't do," the curator told them gently, "the claims tribunal requires documentation..."

"Documentation," echoed Arthur, "but we left in fear of our lives, in the middle of the night... who, in such circumstances, keeps documentation in a crisis?" Then he had another thought, "... Or, I know, look up Mr. Templemann, who sold them to us..."

The curator shook his head. "I'm afraid that we've made many attempts to trace Mr Templemann, the dealer. He was sent east and no one knows what became of him. His gallery is long gone. We've already tried to trace paintings that were sold through him. But there is no paperwork.

That afternoon and the next day, they went from one government office to the next, filling out forms in triplicate at every stop. But no one gave them any hope. "Without proof, anyone could come here claiming to own them." said one official in a jaded tone, "and believe me, they do. You people are not the first."

After a week of frustration and impasse, they accepted defeat and set off back to England. "It makes me so angry," said Ilse, "To know that after all we have gone through, and now they are still doing it. I feel as though it is too much to bear. To know that they have won."

Arthur put his arm round her and she rested her head on his shoulder.

Sleeping back in her own bed at home, Ilse was so exhausted that she fell into the deepest of sleep. And in her sleep, she dreamed that she was walking around the most wonderful garden, quite over-grown and full of flowers. At its centre was a rose bush, smothered in red blossoms. She went over to it and stooped to cup a blossom in her hand, meaning to inhale its fragrance. But, as she did so, the red rose crumbled in her hand, leaving her staring down at a pile of fragrant dust.

"Just like our hopes." said Arthur, when she told him the dream. "Perhaps it's time for us to let go of the past and move on..."

Ilse cocked her head on one side and frowned. She didn't think that that had been the meaning of the dream at all. The dream had stirred some latent memory in her subconscious.

That afternoon, she walked like a dreamer down into the garden and to the overgrown out-house. Inside, it was piled with tea chests and cartons. She pulled off an old tarpaulin, started pulling out boxes, churning up dust and mould. She worked methodically, moving, lifting, dragging everything, piece by piece, to the other wall, aiming to give herself access to the furthest boxes under the window. When she reached the window, she gave a sharp intake of breath, as her eye lit on the item she was seeking. There, in the darkest, dampest corner, on top of some shelving by the window, was a shoebox.

She pulled it out. With trembling hands, lifted the lid. Inside, was a long-stemmed red rose dry as dust. She picked it up, carefully – so carefully. Underneath, was a gold-edged visiting card, written in a gothic hand, *May these pictures bring you great happiness, with kind regards, Heinz Templemann.* Ah, Mr Templemann, that sweet, gallant, old-fashioned gentleman. She lifted up the card and, there it was. The receipt for six oil paintings by Pierre Auguste Renoir, dated July 18th, 1932.

When the euphoria had subsided, Arthur said that evening over dinner, "You know what upsets me. Remember '*La Seine*' – the one the SS man took to get us out – how do we ever trace that. He changed the receipt…. the receipt, my God…. the receipt." He stopped talking to allow the thought to penetrate his brain, then with giant strides, half running, he rushed upstairs.

CHAPTER 30

Arthur and Ilse reclined in the back seat of their Wolsley saloon car. It needed to be an important mission to take them into the centre of Manchester. The car shook as it traversed a network of tramlines.

David Goodson, storeman turned driver, crunched into a lower gear and turned his head to apologize. Once in Deansgate, their passage was smoother. As they approached Kendal Milne, Harrods of the North, Arthur asked the driver to slow down. He would never miss an opportunity to study the fashion windows in transit.

The vehicle behind did not appreciate the go-slow and sounded an impatient horn. "Keep yer hair on," David muttered under his breath. In retaliation, traffic lights brought them to a complete halt. They turned towards Cross Street and into South King Street.

David had been brought up in the city and knew how to approach their destination. He turned again to ask his passengers the number.

Arthur did not need to consult his papers, "Number 126. It's just there on the right."

The car shuddered as they crossed the tramlines again.

"We'll be about forty-five minutes," he said, as he helped Ilse from the car.

They had some difficulty spotting the sign they sought. In earlier days it had been bright gold, embossed. Now it was covered in grime and dust, devoid of polish. The letters were barely discernable:

Levy & Cohen,
Solicitors. Commissioner of Oaths,
2nd Floor.

Mr Levy himself opened the door and ushered them into his modest one room office, dispensing with any delay in the two- chair waiting area. The small office was littered with files, documents and legal papers. If his working area was small, it was more than compensated by the warmth of his effusive greeting.

"How nice to see you again, Mr. & Mrs Grunfeld," he said, showing them to the two chairs that he had only just cleared of papers in readiness for their visit. "Do sit down. I see you are both well."

They exchanged a few more pleasantries before considering the subject matter.

Ilse studied the features of the man sitting opposite. She often wondered why her husband insisted upon using him. Surely someone younger would have been more suitable for this Brief, she thought. Bernard Levy was a family man with wisdom and experience etched all over his wizened face. His eyes had lost their clarity, but not his brain. He was a devout member of the Jewish community, whose priorities lay in the service of his people. He must have been well beyond the age of retirement, but enjoyed his work too much to leave it. Arthur had found him to be meticulous and totally reliable on previous Briefs, which had been concluded to his full satisfaction.

"And how can I be of service to you on this occasion?" he enquired.

He balanced his bi-focals precariously on the very tip of his nose. Now, in anticipation of listening rather than reading, he removed them.

Ilse started their story nervously, "You remember our son Nathan.......?"

"Of course I do. Do you not recall – I was at his Bar Mitzvah? A lovely boy and what a voice."

"Well, he's working as an interpreter at the War Trials in Nüremberg, and he's come face to face with Hermann Göring."

"How very disagreeable," the solicitor commented.

"Disagreeable yes," Ilse agreed, "but helpful. You see, Nathan is sure that Göring knows the whereabouts of our stolen Renoir paintings."

Mr Levy raised his eyebrows; he knew all about impressionist paintings and their spectacular rise in value. He said, "What good fortune you have to own such splendid works of art."

Ilse stated the obvious, "And now we want them back."

The old solicitor listened carefully, taking notes, occasionally shaking his head as the story unfolded. He enquired whether there existed any proof of ownership. With some pride, Ilse produced a sealed envelope from her handbag. "It's like God's miracle that we kept and found these papers," she said as she handed him first the Templemann receipt and then unfolded the amended document that the Colonel had written out confirming 'custody' of the four paintings by the 3rd Reich. Arthur had found the document with his Visa and original passport. Ilse shuddered at the sight of the out-stretched Eagle, with swastika below it; it brought back vivid memories of that fateful night.

Mr. Levy unfolded his glasses to study the document. The bridge of his bi-focals found the invisible ridge on the tip of his nose that seemed to keep them in place. Finally he said, "How fortunate we are that the Nazis were so thorough in their paperwork. Thank the Good Lord for that." He folded his hands and looked skywards. He continued, "So the receipt names only four paintings. The fifth, you say, was taken by the Colonel and not receipted."

"That is correct. He wanted no record. It was his price for letting us go."

"Quite so. Its title?"

"*La Seine.*"

There was silence for two minutes while the solicitor considered the matter. Finally, he removed his spectacles to give his verdict. He chose his words carefully. "With the considerable benefit of these papers, my advice to you is, that I should instruct my colleague solicitor in Munich with instructions to instigate immediate and irrevocable steps to recover the four paintings referred to in these documents. I have every confidence that their unquestionable legality will allow us to locate and recover the paintings, wherever they may be. I would suggest we should allow a period of six months before they revert to your possession."

Arthur and Ilse exchanged glances.

"That's wonderful news," Ilse said.

The solicitor continued, "However, I must warn you that the painting taken by the Nazi Colonel," he paused to look at his notes, "'*La Seine*,' will be more difficult to retrieve. We have neither receipt, nor address. Certainly we cannot go through the official channels – but we have other means. We know his name and regiment," he looked again at the document and quoted, "It's signed Fritz Kohler. Our agents will locate him, I do not doubt. If you will grant me powers to take all necessary steps to recover the five paintings, it will be done to the very best of my ability."

"I think that we are happy to do that." Both Arthur and Ilse nodded in approval.

"Then I must raise the question of funding the operation," the solicitor continued.

Arthur interrupted the oncoming financial assessment, "Mr. Levy, the cost is of no consequence. We must get the pictures out of Germany at any cost, and payment of all fees in this matter is guaranteed by me. I will leave you a deposit of £1000 to cover the initial outlay and thereafter, whatever fees are presented."

Mr. Levy thanked him for his assurance and asked if there were any more questions.

"Yes, I would like to say something else." He looked again at Ilse for reassurance and cleared his throat, "the pictures belong to my wife. We have discussed this matter at great length and are quite decided that once they have been recovered, we wish them to be sold at auction in the US, to realize the highest possible price. The full proceeds are to be donated to a charity that will help clothe, feed and rehabilitate Jewish survivors of the Holocaust."

Arthur was overcome by emotion at the memory of the horrendous pictures shown on TV. Their gesture was a 'Thank you God' that they were spared a similar fate.

CHAPTER 31

Fritz Kohler looked well in his retirement.

Now in his early eighties, veteran of two world wars, he felt privileged to enjoy the good things in life. Although overweight, his chins falling below his neck, he still managed the demeanour of a military man.

Since the passing of his wife, he lived alone in the former family home that they had shared for fifty-two years. He arranged his days' activities with military precision, even to the extent of posting a notice on the wall, on which he accounted his programme for every waking hour. From 7 – 9 pm daily, it was a regular slot; he played records on his radiogram. It was 8:30 pm and he was conducting 'his' orchestra against the new Furtwängler recording of Brahms' 1st symphony. He cursed as an unexpected knock on the door spoilt his concentration. He hated to interrupt the music, so let it play while he answered the door.

Two men casually dressed in sweaters and jeans stood in the doorway. Said one, "You Fritz Kohler, former SS Colonel?"

He was giving nothing away.

"Who wants to know? What's your business?"

Without answering, the two men forced their entrance, pushing him aside and slammed the door behind them.

The Colonel said acidly, "I do not remember inviting you into my home."

Ignoring the rebuke, the two men pushed their way into the living room, where the record was still playing at high volume. Said one of them, "You like Brahms, do you?"

It was a conciliatory remark, intended to put the Colonel at ease. He replied, "That is my choice for tonight's concert."

"Sorry to spoil your enjoyment, but please turn it off."

Dutifully he went to the radiogram and lifted the arm off the record. The silence was eerie.

"I'm Moshe," said the senior of the two, "this is Danny."

Whilst the two men looked around the room, the Colonel said, "Would you kindly inform me what this is all about? Otherwise I shall call the Police."

Gruffly, Moshe pushed him into one of his armchairs. It was the first act of aggression. The Colonel became aware that this was no social visit and that he would have little chance to call for help. Whilst he was seated, the men were examining contents of the room with meticulous care. The furniture was dated and had seen a lot of living. Some ornaments decorated the table and mantle-piece. The front wall was dominated by a large reproduction of the Van Gogh '*Sunflowers.*'

Moshe said, looking at it, "So you like Brahms and the impressionists. Very nice."

His eyes focussed on a photograph of the Colonel in uniform. "You do look handsome; the SS uniform really does something for you. I love to see a man in uniform, with all those medals and Swastikas." With icy coolness, "lovely, really lovely."

The Colonel sounded desperate, "Look, please tell me what you want. I will be pleased to help you all I can."

Moshe ignored the plea. He said to Danny, "Look around the house. See what you can find. I'll watch him."

He then looked carefully at the Van Gogh reproduction. It was suspiciously large and covered most of the wall. He lifted the bottom, peered beneath it and finally took it from its peg. He found what he wanted; the markings of a smaller painting that had been hanging there before. He noted the small hole, obviously caused by the screw that had hung it. He rubbed a wet finger over the dust and scratch marks that remained, which told him that the former picture had not been long removed.

Whilst he was examining these telltale signs, he observed from the corner of his eye that the old man, still cowering in the armchair, had moved his body within reach of a brass poker that lay by the fireside.

When Moshe's back was purposefully turned, he grabbed the poker with speed of movement that belied the old man's age and size. He held it above him ready to inflict a major strike.

But Moshe saw it coming and was one step ahead. He deflected the arm that brandished the poker and delivered a stunning blow on the Colonel's chin. As he fell to the ground, he received two further punches to the head. The blood was pouring from his nose and he was holding his ear in pain, whilst making pitiful noises of anguish.

Alarmed by the commotion, Danny rushed into the room. "Everything OK?" he asked.

"Fine. He tried to hit me with the poker. Silly bastard. Find anything?"

"Nothing. Only a few pictures of naked women, if you're interested."

"Another time," said Moshe. "Take a look at the wall. Looks conclusive. That's where it was alright. But where the hell is it now? I think our friend will be pleased to tell us by the time we've finished with him."

With scant respect for the Colonel's condition, they dragged him off the floor and threw him onto the settee. The floor where he had lain was covered in blood, still dripping from his face. They 'roughed' him up with punches to the body and slaps to his cheeks. He was in no shape to offer any resistance. He made whimpering noises, but was too proud to ask for mercy. Finally Moshe stepped aside and with clenched teeth said, "Now tell us Herr Kohler…. just cast your mind back…. you were on duty at Moers, exit point to Holland…. A Jewish family fell into your clutches trying to leave the country…. you illegally took their Renoir painting…. and now that you've been enjoying it for ten years or more, it's time to give it back…. understand?"

A look of comprehension came over the Colonel's face.

Moshe continued, "Now your choice is quite a simple one. Either you give us that painting or we kill you. One Nazi more or less means nothing to us. You've tormented enough of our people and revenge is sweet. It is quite obvious that the painting was hanging here before the Van Gogh. Where it is now?"

He pulled a revolver from his pocket, cocked it and slowly pointed it at the old man. There was no response. Looking at his watch, he said, "You have twenty seconds to tell us Mr. SS Colonel or I shall blow your brains out."

The old man stirred from his prone position to remove a handkerchief from his pocket to nurse his wounds. He was playing for time to think.

127

"I trust you will allow your prisoner to dress his wounds."

Still looking at his watch, "In another ten seconds, you will have a bigger wound to dress."

It was quite obvious that the old man was going to talk, but he wanted to retain his dignity. He whimpered, "It was a gift. They gave it to me as a present."

"Yeah," he sneered, "Father Christmas came early, did he?"

"Come on now, time is running out."

Moshe rested the weapon menacingly against the Colonel's skull. A sharp twist of the barrel against his withered skin produced no response. But he winced in agony when the gun was placed against the gash on his cheek still oozing blood. The pain registered the futility of further resistance. Stumbling over his words, his head bowed in abject surrender, he said quietly, "If you would like to move the table to the side…. remove the carpet…. lift the loose floor board."

No further directions were required.

The painting, wrapped in rough sackcloth was carefully lifted from its hiding place. The two men undid it and stood it on the mantle-piece. They examined it from all angles. It was undamaged and spectacular.

Moshe prepared to send a message on his walkie-talkie.

"Message to Simon Wiesberg. Agent 417 calling. Mission accomplished. Over."

On June 27th, 1947, Arthur and Ilse received a letter, which bore stamps of the United States. It read:

Dear Mr. & Mrs. Grunfeld,

We are pleased to inform you that your five Renoir paintings achieved record prices at yesterday's auction.

They realized a total of 2.2 million US Dollars (less 10% commission).

We would like to express our gratitude for this outstanding donation. It will be put to excellent use in supporting Jewish survivors of the Holocaust.

Sincerely yours,

Margaret Waller,

Secretary

Rehabilitation of Camp Survivors Trust.

Great Art

CHAPTER 32

I had not heard from Nathan for nearly ten years after these momentous historical events, so it was a pleasant surprise when a sealed envelope with beautifully handwritten address arrived in the post. It contained a card with gold serrated edging and embossed wording to match.

Sydney and Judith Weinstock
Request the pleasure of your company
On the occasion of the wedding of their daughter
Hannah to Nathan Grunfeld.
RSVP

I reflected on his good fortune with some envy. He was heir to a brilliant business and now a wife, no doubt attractive and from a respectable family. There would be children and a luxurious home, opulently furnished; money, no object. He was a lucky fellow.

After Nüremberg, I had returned to my original base at British Forces Network, the Radio Station, with the intention of only staying for a few months, while I prepared for demob and learnt my trade. The major impediment was money, or lack of it. I had neither home nor capital and was totally dependent on my weekly wage. The environment was comfortable and I was soon kept busy writing and introducing too many programmes to think about furthering my career in the UK.

Heidi, my girlfriend from Nüremberg, came over to see me quite frequently. She had put on weight and now looked quite voluptuous. Clearly, she was looking for a husband, but after Gisela, I had my reservations. She was impressed with my work and I used to slip her into the studio where she would sit the other side of the microphone and pull funny faces at me whilst I ad-libbed. She was with me one night, whilst I was DJ'ing 'Spin with the Stars', a sixty-minute programme at midnight. She sneezed noisily in the middle of an announcement.

I had always been taught to draw attention to any fluff or irregularity, on air rather than hide it. "Gesundheit," I said.

"Oh, Mein Gott," she exclaimed, "Entschuldigung. I am so sorry. Wie furchtbar." She emitted a mixture of pigeon English and German.

I was then obliged to introduce her to my listeners and the rest of the programme became a double act, joking about her English and her very presence in the studio.

Listeners, both English and German, liked what they heard and wanted more. Even the papers picked up the story with a picture of us. Heidi was officially booked for a weekly slot as co-host. She received a small pay package, enough to commute or stay over and became something of a celebrity. Her trademark remained her unintentionally hilarious translation from the idioms of one language to the other.

As a result, she was offered a record series of her own with Nord West Deutscher Rundfunk, which was a great success and led to some TV bookings. As it was all thanks to me, I was offended but not unhappy, when she informed me that she had entered into a relationship with Billy Bentley, who was a pop star of dubious repute. The papers published the story and so ended our relationship.

Shortly afterwards my solicitor rang me with good news. He had concluded a deal with the German Government. I was one of the first to receive compensation: it totalled about sixty thousand pounds. With this amount safely in hand, I had the confidence to leave BFN and take my chances in the UK.

On arrival in London, I made two acquisitions. The first was the outright purchase of a small three-bedroom house in Chelsea in a charming street just off Kings Road. The second was a theatrical agent to get me work.

Eric began arranging auditions for me, some of which yielded the occasional booking. But it soon became clear that, for the time being, I could not expect a regular income and work.

I was not good at being inactive and, now that I had some capital, I turned my thoughts as to how I could invest in some business venture, which would keep me busy whilst I waited for radio work to materialise.

One of my squash partners was Otto Marcus. He was a slight man of athletic build, sparkling eyes that were as quick to see an opening around the squash court, as to pick a good business deal. His King's English was dubious and his education might well have been hi-jacked at an early age in favour of some scheme or other. But whatever shortcomings there might have been in this area, were compensated by enthusiasm for any project he undertook and total honesty.

He had been, and still was, trying to make ends meet, with a small art business in Hampstead, which he had inherited from his parents. He sold prints, cheap originals, cards and any other items that could loosely be categorized as Art accessories. However, it was his December trading, when he sold Christmas cards that kept his head above water. The premises were larger than required for this painstaking business and I had visions of tearing out all the old fashioned shelving and fixtures, creating a beautiful open space, painting the walls white and converting it into an art gallery, featuring the work of unknown artists. For, whilst in Cologne, I had become very interested in modern art.

I struck a deal with Otto to buy a fifty percent partnership for ten thousand pounds, this money funding the conversion I had in mind. Such was the success of the gallery that five years later, I was to buy him out for the sum of one hundred thousand pounds. I was fully occupied with this project, preparing our first one-man-show, when Nathan's wedding invitation arrived.

It was an emotional moment when I met him again for the first time since Nüremberg. He was still living in the first floor flat above his parents' home. I was quite shocked to see how much weight he had put on. He had more than a paunch, and his face was fuller. His hair had grown prematurely grey in patches and some crow's feet had appeared about his eyes.

As we embraced in the warm friendship that we had always enjoyed, I complimented him on how well he looked and relatively unchanged.

He was less gentle. As he looked me up and down, he said, "Hair's gone. A few wrinkles; a double chin to be proud of. Otherwise OK." Nathan could always be relied upon to be more colourful than tactful.

We had lots of news to exchange. Nathan had been appointed MD of Grunfelds and now, it seemed, spent much of his time chasing turnover, currently standing at two point five million, and trying to keep profit ratio in line. Sadly, his father had suffered a heart attack, from which he was recovering only slowly. Nathan had met Hannah through the synagogue, "She's a lovely girl from a very highly respected family," he said. "You'll meet her tomorrow and see for yourself. She's lovely."

Reading between the lines, I gained the impression that this was a marriage of convenience more than passion.

"Where will you be living?" I asked, wondering whether his bachelor flat would be adequate to the needs of a married couple.

"We're going to honeymoon in Barbados and then move back here for a short time. We've already bought a great house quite near, which Hannah will decorate and furnish. I'll keep my eye on it of course," he added, a little pompously I thought.

Then I asked the question, most on my mind, "What happened to the Renoirs? Are they here? I'd love to see them."

"So would I," said Nathan, "You wouldn't believe it. After all the fuss getting them back, my father wouldn't tolerate having them in the house, because of where they'd been. Sort of tainted. He didn't want to be looking at what Göring and his cronies had been looking at. He did something amazingly generous – donated the pictures to the Jewish survivors' rehabilitation trust. It made him happy, a sort of thank you, God, for getting us out. Got a big write-up in the Jewish Chronicle."

"What a wonderful gesture," I said, "they must have sold for a fortune."

Throughout the conversation, my eyes had been riveted to the facing wall, on which were hanging seven paintings of varying size, by L.S. Lowry. Of course, Nathan had told me of his great love of this artist's work in Nüremberg. Although I had read about him and seen prints, I had never seen an original.

The phone rang. Nathan excused himself, picked it up, began talking last minute wedding details with the caller who was obviously Hannah, his wife-to-be.

I took the opportunity to walk over and study each of the canvases in turn. I was impressed. I loved the texture, the colours, the aspects of industry, and the sheer pace of the figures rushing about. The little dogs, the buildings; they were all so primitive, yet realistic.

When he returned, he said, "She's worrying herself to death about all the arrangements. I have to reassure her it will be alright on the night."

Still staring at the pictures I said, "They're fabulous, I love them."

His face lit up, "Now you can understand why I have become so infatuated with them? Some are like Impressionists. Look at that antique sky... Hundreds of people on the move... I spend hours just staring at them. It's become my favourite past-time," he moved to one in particular, "Look, this is my favourite, *Industrial Scene*. Come closer... See. It's only a blur. Now step away a few paces, it's a whole town in the distance," pointing, "there's a church steeple, buildings, chimneys. They are so brilliant." Nathan got excited whenever he talked about his Lowrys. "You know, I've met him quite a few times now. You'd never think from looking at him that he was an artist. A very down-to-earth old-fashioned guy. Lives alone. A recluse. And comes up with these brilliant paintings."

Nathan had been increasing his collection, whenever the opportunity arose. Not long ago he had bought *A Square in Lytham* from his local gallery. It showed figures in immaculate detail, which stood about six inches high.

"I envy you these pictures," I said, "they're stunning. How much did they set you back?"

Nathan remembered the price he had paid for each.

"Well, I've got to tell you, this one near bankrupted me. It was my first. I was a teenager. Tom, they wouldn't let me out of the shop until I'd given them – five pounds! But – the next was twenty-five, then fifty, then seventy-five. Now they're asking £250 for them, no less. God only knows if ever I could get my money back. But, who cares? I love them."

"You've got a lovely collection here. I'd love to buy one or two for my new house."

"Well you may be able to meet the old boy tomorrow. I asked him to come to the wedding weeks ago. He declined of course. I tried again more recently. He still said no. He's a bit shy and hates crowds. Then I had a really good idea. I commissioned him to do a painting of the wedding. I said it would be wonderful to have one of his canvasses hung importantly in our new house to remind us of the occasion. Well, he sort of said he might and left it at that. He may come, but I wouldn't put money on it. We'll have to wait and see."

CHAPTER 33

L. S. Lowry at a Jewish wedding! A fish out of water, indeed. I spotted him the moment he set foot in the suite. He had missed the sit-down dinner and crept in surreptitiously, shoulders hunched forward in a half-hearted attempt to escape notice, when the dancing and other celebrations were at their height. He was wearing a clean grey suit, with stiff-collared white shirt and black tie. He sat in the first chair he came to at an empty table and took immediate refuge behind a large pad he had bought with him. He soon became engrossed and recorded by pencil what he saw.

Nathan went over to greet him and I saw Mr. Lowry hand over a small square package, which I assumed to be a drawing. They shook hands, and Nathan beckoned a waiter to bring a glass of champagne and a plate of petit fours.

I intended to introduce myself to the artist when there was a lull in the music. However, just now, as the dancing got to its most uninhibited, two ladies of Rubenesque proportions, not young, but with bosoms well on display, jiggled over to him, moving to the music and shouting above the din, "Come on Mr. Lowreh."

He mumbled inaudibly, "Aw look, I don't dance much mesel," but they were insistent. "Boot everyone's dancin', Mr Lowreh. You've got to join in," To my dismay, they each took an arm, pulled him to his feet and steered him to the dancing area. He did not look at all comfortable, but bravely stood his ground, looking sheepish, arms by his side, vaguely tapping his feet in some sort of rhythm that only he could have understood.

As Nathan danced by with his new wife in his arms, he shouted, "Good to see you on the floor, Mr. Lowry. You just enjoy yourself."

"Thanks," replied the recluse, grimly, "Ay, well, ah'm doin' mah best."

I wandered over to pay my respects to Nathan's parents. Arthur

135

looked frail but he was still a handsome man, with his grey hair brushed back and his twinkling blue eyes. That Ilse was Nathan's mother there could be no doubt. They had the same mannerisms, the same profile. She had shoulder length hair that flicked up at the ends, making her look half her age. They were an elegant, distinguished couple.

We chatted about the war and the part that Nathan and I had played in Nuremberg. I said, "I followed the story of your Renoirs from beginning to end. I'd like to congratulate you on your wonderful gesture."

"It was hard to get them back," said Ilse, "but very satisfying to give them away again."

When the music came to its next rest, I saw the ladies return Mr Lowry to the table, whence they had so unceremoniously gathered him up.

I allowed him five minutes to recover then strolled over and introduced myself, "How d'you do, Mr. Lowry," I said, shaking his hand. He looked mystified.

"I saw some of your oils at Nathan's flat. I loved them so much, that I was wondering if I could buy one or two for my new home in Chelsea."

But Mr. Lowry had passed the stage where he was happy to get a few pounds at the discretion of the buyer. He said, "Well, look, it's lahk this. Ah've joost signed oop with a gallery in London and, seein' as you live ther, that'd be best place to go. Ah've joost sent 'em ten canvases. Real good 'uns. They're in Bruton Street. Called Lefèvres."

Plan one had failed. I was hoping to get an invitation to his studio while in Manchester. I tried again, "It would be excellent if I could have taken one home with me. Have you got any available?"

"Ah'm workin' on two or three at the moment, but they're not yet finished." Quite clearly he didn't need money, nor was he interested in making a sale from home. He was such an intriguing character, totally down to earth without any artistic temperament that I was keen to find out more about him.

I hit on an idea as we were talking and explored it, "I have some connections to BBC Television and I believe that a programme, showing your work and background could be very worthwhile and of great interest to the viewers."

You would have thought that such an offer of nationwide, free publicity would have evoked some enthusiasm, at least, if not excitement. But he expressed only guarded interest, asking, "Well, 'ow long would it ta-ake?"

"Probably a day, maybe two..." knowing full well that it would be more, if we were to record a thirty minute feature.

"Well, ah suppose yer c'd ta-ake mah phone number. And yer c'd ring if yer wanted ter discoos it further?"

I took down his number and gave him my card. "I'll be in touch," I said "and I'll go to Lefevres to have a look."

We shook hands and parted. I had used this ploy genuinely at BFN where I had been in a position to implement my proposal. Here, it would not be quite so easy. But I had met a BBC features producer whom I might be able to persuade and I thought I would give it my best shot on my return to London.

I caught up with Nathan, between dances with Hannah. She cut a lovely figure in her white and pink brocade dress. She was attractive, but not beautiful with a kind face and an engaging smile, her blondish hair arranged in an elaborate chignon over head. I assessed her at once as a charming, well-groomed wife who would stand by her man throughout his life.

"What a wonderful do," I shouted to her above the music.

"It's gone really well," she shouted back, smiling, a little flushed by all the activity and very merry. "We're so happy. And looking forward to Barbados."

Now a guest came up and claimed her. As she danced off, I turned to Nathan, "Congratulations, she's lovely."

We sat down and I told him of my meeting with Mr. Lowry.

"Yes, he's getting very cagey now. Doesn't like to sell direct any more. Obviously, he gets a better price selling through Lefevre and every sale helps build his reputation with them."

"I'm surprised they sell in London. After all, they are very northern pictures."

"He's beginning to take off nation-wide and news travels fast."

"I'm curious," I said, "I saw him give you a package. Have you opened it yet?" Nathan had placed it on the top table, unopened.

"Would you like me to?"

We walked over and he opened the package. It was not a drawing, nor even a watercolour. It was a full coloured miniature oil, showing yachts in the sunset. No figures for once, but the sky and sea, blending in beautiful auburn colours. It was a painting that could have come from the easel of the finest Impressionist painter.

The back was inscribed, *To Nathan and Hannah, wishing you every happiness*, and signed, L.S.L.

Nathan and I exchanged glances.

"Mazeltov," I said, "The luck of the Irish."

That little gift would, one day, be valued at twenty thousand pounds.

Nathan now had a head start of eight Lowrys. I would have to get going to catch him.

CHAPTER 34

I returned to my Chelsea home full of ideas. The meeting with Mr. Lowry, and Nathan's beautiful paintings had inspired me. My first move was to ring the Lefèvre gallery to establish if, indeed, they had some Lowry paintings to show me. I spoke to Mr. Cadogen, who had such a heavy accent that I could barely understand him. But I gathered that of ten canvasses submitted, two had already sold and a further two were under offer. They were going like 'hot cakes' he said, and if I was serious in wanting one, I should not delay. We fixed an appointment for 2 pm that day.

I relished the walk down Bond Street, looking at the boutiques and the pretty girls, so decided to leave the car behind and take the tube.

Mr. Cadogan greeted me effusively. Complete with monocle, pin stripes and a spotted bow tie, he was the very caricature of an art dealer. How different he was, I thought, from his artist client.

It did not take me long to locate the Lowrys. The two best were hanging side by side in the main gallery. Two further, in the back room and three very nice drawings were not displayed, resting against the side wall. It was not a major decision. The two hanging side by side in the gallery were superb, like twins that should not be separated. I decided to have them both, irrespective of price. In addition, I felt they would make a good investment.

The Junction was a typical Lowry. It showed a street winding upwards, with houses either side and chimneys in the background. It was a very cheerful, optimistic picture with a lot of red and the familiar grey sky. There were figures in the foreground, quite large and in detail, and going up the street in decreasing size. The other was called *The Bus Stop*. It showed eleven figures, cowering under multi-coloured umbrellas, standing in the rain, waiting for a bus. You could almost feel the discomfort and dampness as they waited.

I felt sure that Nathan would have approved my selection.

I gave no indication to Mr. Cadogan that I had already made up my mind to have the pair. I asked their price. He consulted his price list, ran his finger down a column, and finally told me that *The Junction* would be six hundred guineas and *The Bus Stop* four hundred guineas. I sighed wistfully when I heard the price, implying it was way above my expectations. Mr Cadogan hovered around me as I explored other exhibits, particularly the three pencil drawings, one of which, called *The Tree*, was exceptional. I enquired its price. Eighty guineas, I was told. The more I examined it, the better I liked it. The tree was in the centre, surrounded by a fence, paving stones, with good-size figures and in the background, rows of houses and a factory. It was a brilliant composition.

I asked Mr. Cadogan what the price would be, if I purchased the two oils and the drawing. He scurried into the back office, excited at the prospect of selling three, obviously to ask his superior, what sort of a discount could be offered for such a significant transaction. He came back after a short while with an offer to reduce each one by ten guineas, so that the total expenditure would amount to one thousand and fifty guineas.

I pretended to think about it, "Sorry that's a bit too much for me. My best offer for the three pictures would be one thousand pounds – not guineas."

"That is a bit drastic," he said, "but I will enquire."

It took another fifty pounds to clinch the deal. I paid by cheque and the three pictures were to be delivered to my home within seven days, presumably to clear the cheque before delivery. This did not worry me unduly and I was happy to have concluded the transaction. Before I left, I collected a catalogue and photographs of all the Lowrys' that had passed through their hands. As I walked to the tube station, I thought to myself; I've got three, only five needed and I'm up with Nathan.

I was friendly at the time with a girl producer in BBC TV. Her name was Jenny Marshall and she had aspirations of becoming a features director. I always felt that she was keener on me, than I on her. I rang her to say, "I've got a proposal to make you."

"Sounds good," she said.

We made a date for dinner the following week. I picked her up from her flat in Chiswick, and was pleasantly surprised to see how pretty and feminine she looked. I had only seen her in office garb, which did not do her justice. Now she wore a denim mini skirt, way above the knees and a sloppy sweater that hung loosely around her hips and arms. Her shapely legs were bare. She smiled sweetly on my arrival and we kissed politely on each cheek. She reeked of nicotine.

Before, during and after dinner at a restaurant in Chelsea called 'Au père de Nico,' she must have gone through ten cigarettes. After the meal is one thing, but between courses and even mouthfuls... I managed to refrain from comment.

I outlined my 'proposal.' She had not heard of L.S. Lowry and so I related how I had met the man, what a strange fish he was and how I had completely fallen for his art. "And now Lefèvres have them. I think he's going to become big. He paints Northern scenes, but even in London, people are buying them." I waved away her smoke with my hand, "I think he could be the subject of a very interesting little feature, directed by Jenny Marshall and introduced by yours truly."

"It sounds fascinating," she said, "Just the sort of thing BBC 2 likes doing, but there's not much money around at the moment, and the schedules are pretty full up. I'd like to see the paintings and form an opinion."

I showed her the catalogues and the photos first, then took her home to show her the real thing. She was impressed. She said she would give it her best shot but couldn't promise a thing. We stayed talking for hours about how a programme could be best handled and by the time the eighteenth cigarette had been stubbed into the ashtray and the second bottle of wine consumed, it was nearly one o'clock.

"Good God," she exclaimed, "I've got a meeting at the office in eight hours."

"If you'd you like to stay over, you're very welcome." I offered. "I'll cook you breakfast in the morning and you can go straight to the office from here."

"I haven't got a thing with me. Not even a toothbrush."

"That's no problem, I'll lend you mine."

It reminded me of a line from a play by Somerset Maugham,

141

'*The Constant Wife*,' that I had recently seen: '*The acid test of love is whether you can share the same toothbrush.*'

I lead her to the bedroom upstairs and kissed her on the mouth. The smell of nicotine was overpowering, but I persevered until we reached such a pitch of passion that it ceased to bother me and we even managed to get some sleep as well. We rose in good time for her early meeting. I drove her to her office and as we parted, affectionately. I said, "It's been a wonderful night, meeting you properly." and almost in the same breath, "When do you think I will hear from you about the programme?"

"Look, don't bank on it. It's a fifty to one chance."

"I'll put a fiver on your making it."

She blew me a kiss as she went.

I went to the chemist to buy myself a new toothbrush.

CHAPTER 35

Looking for Mr. Lowry's home, I went down the Stalybridge Road twice searching for 'The Elms', in Mottram-in-Longdendale. No one could be blamed for missing it first time round or for hesitating to stop outside the second time.

An unprepossessing, grim-looking house of dull brick and slate. From the outside, it had the appearance of traditional two up, two down. The windows were rectangular and showed little trace of having ever been cleaned. The garden was a shambles, heavily overgrown with weeds and foliage. It was clear that Mr. Lowry was no lover of house or garden maintenance.

He greeted me at the door without too much enthusiasm and said ... dryly, "so yer found it a'reet?"

"Yes, fine," I lied.

"Yer'd best coom in, then." He ushered me into his living room which was reserved, as he told me, "for important visitors only."

He sat me down on one of the two armchairs in the front room and he took the other opposite. There was a large table in the centre of the room, littered with papers. There were canvasses piled in one corner and a sideboard cluttered with clocks, portraits and bric-a-brac. The walls were depressingly dark, enriched by the volume of paintings and portraits, not all his own, that hung on them. The armchairs were threadbare and the furniture and ambience of the room might have been more appropriate to the previous century. Nevertheless, it was homely and the present occupant clearly felt comfortable in these surroundings.

Face to face with him, I studied his features. He was tall with thick grey hair, parted on the left. His nose was prominent. He had the hands of a workman and, even though he had spruced himself up for the interview, there were traces of paint on his fingers. He was a very ordinary man that would not stand out in a crowd. He spoke with a strong Northern accent and there could be no mistaking his humble origin. He wore the same black suit and tie, with waistcoat, that he had had on for the wedding, presumably his 'special occasion' outfit.

We were discussing the interview when Jenny Marshall and her three-man crew arrived. Suddenly the place was overcrowded. The true professional she was, it did not take her long to work out the format. It would be Mr. Lowry and I in conversation in the two armchairs and whilst we spoke, the camera would pan around the room and show in close-up some completed pictures. We would then adjourn to his back room, the studio, and watch him physically create a canvas and fill it with his figures, dogs and mills. To show the artist at work in his normal surrounding was, Jenny felt, by far the best way to etch his profile.

I began, "It's very kind of you to let me see your home, Mr Lowry. It looks very comfortable if I may say so. I see a lot of interesting things here."

"It maht look nice to you, but ah ha-ate it. It's all the things I didn't want. Always wanted big airy rooms with high ceilings and plenty of spa-ace to put things, not this God-forsaken doomp. Y'knaw, if ah could, ah'd leave tomorrer."

"What stops you?" I asked.

"So much stuff 'ere. Joost look around. It'd ta-ake a fleet of lorries and an army of removal men to shift. Ah've got so mooch work t'do, if ah had to move, ah'd grind to a halt. When mah moother died, in 1939, ah had to put all her belongings somewhere and this was the only pla-ace, y'knaw?"

"And the clocks? Between the hall and in here, there must be about eight of them?"

"Well, now, they were my fa-ather's big interest. He used t'collect all types of clocks, 'e did, in 'is da-ay. Oil 'em up, ta-ake 'em t'bits, put 'em back together again, listen to the chimes. Used t'loov it, 'e did. When 'e died, in 1932, moother joost took 'em over. What else could she do? And when she died, ah 'ad to do th' same."

There was something so simple, blunt and straightforward about his theories.

"So, your mother played a big role in your life, did she?"

"Oh, ay. Ah loov'd mah moother. It were a terrible shock to me when she died, y'know."

"Did she live to see your success as an artist?"

"Ev'reh picture ah painted, she saw. Soom she li-iked a lot. Oothers she'd sa-ay, 'Lawreh, ah'm not shu-er about this'n. It's not mah fayv'rit'. In them days ah were workin' quite 'ard. Ah 'ad a job. Did mah pictures when ah got 'ome."

"And did you sell them?"

"Not mooch at first. Ah took three of mah oils to a little gallery in Didsbureh and they liked 'em and would pay me a few pounds when they sold 'em. And then ah'd tek in soom more. It took a long ti-ime, y'knaw. Ah could'nt live off it, so ah worked as well. It were very sad. Ah got a woon-man show for first time in 1939, and ah had to prepare twenty-four canvasses. Ah showed moother ev'reh one, but she were poorleh then an' she never got t'see th'show. She were bed-ridden, y'knaw an' she died same year. Very sad, very sad..."

"And how many of the pictures sold from that first show?"

"Ah ca-an't remember that well. Ah don't think any ca-ame back, so they moost have sold soom ti-ime or oother."

"And did that make you a rich man?"

"Yer must be jo-okin'! A few coppers to buy food with. Ah couldn't give oop mah day job on that, y'knaw."

"And what was your day job?"

"Ah were workin' for the Pall Mall property coompany. They own a lot of houses around 'ere and in Pendlebury. And mah job was to collect the rent ev'reh week. Ah went to each house ev'reh week with a little receipt book, collected their pound, or two, an' then did an account to the coompany when ah paid over the mooney."

"I believe you gave that up in 1952. Does that mean you were making enough money to live on by then?"

"Ah were sellin' qui-ite a lot through some folk in London, a gallereh called Lefèvres. And then ah had some commissions, so ah was a-able t'pai-aint full ti-ime."

I thought it appropriate to reveal at this point that I owned some of his pictures. "I went to the gallery and bought three beautiful ones. I'm very happy with them but I paid a thousand pounds for them. Can you see them going up any higher in price?"

Mr. Lowry shook his head; "Ah know nowt about money matters. Ah joost go on pai-aintin', and if folk want to buy 'em it's oop ter th'gallery t'charge what they think."

"I see you have a nice upright there. Can you give us a tune?"

"Ooh, I 'aven't been near a piano for thirteh years. Moother were a lovely player. She could play anything y'knaw? She 'ad all the music and – look, its all here now, piano an' all. She used t'give me lessons as a boy, but now ah wouldn't know one note from t'oother. Mi-ind you, ah li-ike t'listen. You see, over ther is the radiogram and ah li-ike ter have soom music on while ah'm pai-ainting. A nice bit of Bach cantata, or Mozart opera. Ah've got soom ni-ice records."

The cameraman was circling round us, close with his hand-held camera. Jenny was behind him, signalling to me to move to the final segment of the interview.

"Mr. Lowry, I would like our viewers to know how you would spend a typical day..."

"Well, ah doan't know about typical. Ah joost let things 'appen the way they want to, y'knaw? If ah feel li-ike sleepin' on, ah will. If ah feel li-ike paintin' all day, ah will. That's one ni-ice thing about not 'aving a job, y'knaw. Yer can do whatever y'want. But, usually, ah pai-aint in th'morning, then, catch a bus t'Manchester or some-where, and ah'll move around. Ah always 'ave mah sketchbook with me, and if ah see a good subject, ah'll draw it out with pencil an' then work it out in the evenin', y'knaw. Ah'll 'ave mah tea while ah'm out, doan't often eat at home – an' then get back to pai-aintin' in the evenin'. Soom nights ah keep workin' till past midnight, joost how th'mood takes me. Pai-aintin's a wonderful relaxation, y'knaw. Ah can paint without knawing ah'm doing it. T'me it's li-ike, breathin', eatin'. Ah doan't 'ave t'think about it. It joost cooms, y'knaw?"

"How long does it take you to do a canvas?"

"Ah couldn't put a time on it, really. Y'see, ah'll 'ave three or four goin' at same ti-ime. Ah'll put one down and pick anoother oop. Soomti-imes ah'll 'ave it 'ere for over a year before it's finished. Ah li-ike doin' it that way. Yer doan't get ti-ired of any one soobject. Then again, if ah stick wi' a picture and want t'get it done, ah can finish it in a week."

"And when you're not working, how do you spend your leisure time?"

"Ah've got friends ah visit on th'coast and soomti-imes ah stay over and – d'ye knaw what I do? – ah sit and stare at th'sea. Ah can do that all day long. Ah watch th'wa-aves rollin' in, th'tide coomin' and goin'. Th'sea's li-ike the battle of li-ife, y'knaw? Ah loov it. Ah go t'Soonderland. Y'could leave me there fer a month, joost lookin' at it. And ah'll coom back wi' a whole pad full of sketches and loovly air to breathe in. Ah've done some ni-ice pictures ther – and Lytham. Y'knaw, beach scenes, wi' a lot of folk playin' on th'sand."

"And your people – do you see yourself as one of them? A man in a crowd?"

"Look, mah people are real people, y'knaw. Li-ike you an' me. Ah feel li-ike one of them. Ah really do y'knaw? And it's sad t'see them rooshin' around. They're so busy rooshin', they doan't 'ave time t'live. They doan't talk. It's really sad. And ah'm sad, li-ike them. There's a lot of sadness about in th'world, y'knaw. Sad and lonely, that's what mah people are."

"Can you see yourself getting married? That would do away with being lonely. Wouldn't it?"

"D'you really think ah could persuade any lady t'move into this God forsaken doomp?"

"But, if you could, would you like to see it happen?"

"Ah'm a bit old t'cha-ange mah ways now y'knaw."

"If you made money with your paintings, and became quite rich, how would you change your life?"

"'Ow would ah cha-ange mah life? Well, that's a difficult one."

"Well would you move away from here, as you don't seem to like it much?"

"Well, where could ah go, and how could ah move all mah stoof? To answer the question, ah'd 'ave t'keep on pai-aintin', wherever ah was. So, ah suppose ah may as well pai-aint 'ere as anywhere."

"I think our viewers would very much like to see you at work. Could we adjourn to your studio and perhaps you could talk us through one of your canvasses as you do it?"

The camera pans around to show easel with half finished seascape picture. A promenade with a few people on it, more to come, and oceans of sea beyond it leading to a blue/white sky. Canvasses everywhere. On the table, piles leaning against the walls. The floor covered in paint. Mr. Lowry takes off his clean jacket and puts on his work jacket, which is the same; only that it is covered in paint of all colours. He constantly rubs the paint from his hand and fingers onto the jacket, as a cleansing process.

"So this is where it all happens?" I ask, "Now can we see you turning an empty canvas into one of your beautiful paintings?"

"This week ah went to Salford and ca-ame back wi' a few sketches, just an outline. This is the one ah want t'do next."

He picks up his sketchpad and finds the relevant one. "Yer see, it's very rough: here's a shop, steps leadin' up to it. A few people goin' up. This is a pavement leadin' round it. There's large people in foreground just here, then small ones in distance. In the background, houses and chimneys and small figures and then on skyline, the outline of a town, church steeple and more buildings..."

"So at the very start you plan a three dimensional picture?"

"Ay, well it gives me spa-ace and distance y'knaw. Ah li-ike that. So this will be a ni-ice si-ize. Ah'll take a canvas li-ike this one – that's seventeen inches by twenteh – an' put it on th'easel, readeh."

"But that's already got painting on it."

"Aye. I paint 'em first, white all over and bake 'em."

"What d'you mean 'bake?'"

"Well, ah put 'em in th'oven and ah get a real croosty look. Gives me an antique – old – look. Goes well wi' mah style and gives me the affect ah want."

"So – every canvas you do, you paint all over white, then put it in the oven to bake, then paint over the top?"

"Well, not every one, but plenteh. Y'see, mah folk in London said they could sell 'em better with whi-ite background. Y'knaw, not so da-ark as ah used t'do in them olden da-ays. Well now, lets get sta-arted."

He looks instantly at ease as he becomes immersed in the tools of his trade.

"We have shop here in centre... outline in black...red brick for building and chimney... now some folk goin' up steps... not too big 'cos they're not foreground... now bigger folk at front... an' a dog or two... put the pavement around the shop..."

As he speaks, he draws the lines with deft authority. He knows exactly the effect he wants to achieve and where his figures should be placed. As we watch, the central subject of the picture is taking shape.

Jenny and I sit viewing the rough cut of the film on an editing machine. The picture fades out and the background music of a Bach cantata that we can only hear faintly, is brought up to full volume to indicate the passage of time. As it fades, we watch Mr. Lowry still at work, but now the picture is all but finished. The shop is now fully coloured. There are people milling around the scene of different dimensions. Behind the shop, there are medium sized houses and people, but the pièce de resistance is the magnificent industrial scene in the background. It is no more than a shadow close up, but stand a few steps away, and you can discern a whole dormant city. A masterpiece, if I ever saw one. On screen, I lift it off the easel and study it at arm's length.

I turn to the master and say, "Mr. Lowry. You are a genius." And I meant it. "What are you going to call it?"

"How about '*Shops and People in Salford.*'"

"That's a lovely name. Thank you so much for letting us watch this work of art being created. It's magnificent. We love your work and I'm sure we will be seeing a lot more of it in the future."

"Aye. Thanks."

I shake his hand firmly.

The final shot, perhaps a little disrespectfully, is of me, looking at my hand with paint on it, and rubbing it furiously on a nearby towel.

CHAPTER 36

Through the seventies and early eighties, Nathan and I were in friendly competition to acquire the best Lowrys. Working together, we covered every major auction – Sotheby's, Christies, Phillips, Bonhams... But soon, the prices began to spiral out of control, leaving our bidding hands paralysed by the alarming increases.

There were gasps of incredulity when *Daisy Nook*, arguably the finest Lowry of all time, with a wealth of fine detail, vibrant colours, heaving with activity, was sold for a record seventeen thousand. Nathan and I were too stunned by the rapid escalation to even enter the bidding. However, at that same Sotheby's auction, I was successful in buying *A Street in Clitheroe* for four thousand pounds and Nathan bought *Crime Lake* for seven thousand. These prices seemed inordinately high at the time, but were to rise steeply year by year, as collectors and dealers vied with each other to buy the best pieces. Even drawings and single-figure oils were reaching hitherto unheard of figures.

What would dear old Mr. Lowry have thought were he still alive? If such wealth had come to him within his lifetime, would he have, at last, moved house? Experts believed it was only a question of time before a Lowry reached the million pound mark. At these levels, it became an investment market rather than collectors', and Nathan and I concluded that it would hardly be possible to enlarge our collections further.

It was not unusual to be offered Lowrys for sale privately. One day in June, I received a rather cryptic phone call from an unknown person, who introduced himself as Carl Fisher. The voice was gruff, the speech uneducated, "I believe you got some Lowrys," he began.

"What makes you think that?" I asked, cautiously, wondering how he had got hold of my number.

He mentioned the name of a dealer in Bond Street. "If you're interested, I got a terrific one to sell."

"What is it?" I asked.

"Its a major piece. A good size with a lot of figures. Twenty by twenty-four. He done it in '61. It's a smasher."

"What's it called?" I persisted.

"Don't wanna give too many details right now. On account of the bank having it. Know what I mean?"

I could only guess. "You have a Polaroid of it?" I asked.

"A Polaroid wouldn't do it no justice," he replied, "It's a terrific example of his oeuvre," he pronounced the word carefully, as though he had been trained to say it, "I don't want to hawk it round. If yer wanna see it, you need to come to my premises. I'm based in Hartlepool."

I was quite intrigued by all this cloak and dagger stuff. It would not be the first time I had spent a day travelling to see a painting.

"How much is it?" I asked.

"I'm asking a million for it."

His answer stunned me into silence. At that price, the painting had to be *Daisy Nook* at least, or something even more spectacular. I was curious to see it. "That sounds steep for a Lowry, Mr. Fisher," I said, "He hasn't made that price so far..." But how many times had I said that in the past and been proved wrong? "It would have to be something exceptional. I'd need to know more..."

"Believe me," he broke in, "it's exceptional alright. This is a Lowry ter die for."

I discussed the offer with Nathan. He, too, had received a call from Mr Fisher. I rang the dealer that the man had mentioned. "Never heard of him," he said, "Besides, we never give names out. Must have got hold of a mailing list from somewhere."

Curiosity finally got the better of us and we arranged to meet him the following week. I travelled down on the train and Nathan picked me up from Hartlepool station. The road we sought was nearby. It was decidedly the wealthy end of town. Large four story Victorian houses were on either side of the road, most standing in one or two acres of land.

Carl Fisher greeted us at the door. He was in his late thirties, handsome but with eyes set a little too far apart. Designer suit, Jermyn Street shirt and tie. Nathan and I were more casual in jeans and t-shirts. He showed us into a large sitting room, with high ceiling, sparsely furnished with junky armchairs and settee and very plain chairs around a wooden table. There was a kitchen area in the corner. The walls were bare. The carpet hadn't seen a Hoover for a while.

Mr. Fisher made small talk about the weather and how pleasant it was to live in Hartlepool during the summer. We were waiting to get the pleasantries over and to be taken to the merchandise when the door opened.

Standing in the doorway was a woman so beautiful, that she took my breath away. She was tall with blondish shoulder-length hair, a pale translucent complexion, and the sculptured cheekbones of a model, full lips, glossed in pink. She wore slacks and sweater, high-heeled sandals on bare feet. She was curvy rather than model thin.

"This is my partner, Patsy," said Mr Fisher.

She smiled. Her cool blue eyes met mine and a frisson went through me as though I had been given an electric shock. "Hope your journey hasn't been too hellish." she said. Her voice was upper middle class English, educated, confident in any situation. "It's so humid. Can I get you something to drink? Tea, coffee, mineral water...?"

"A coffee, please." Suddenly I was in no hurry to get the business over with.

Whether she was his business partner or his lover or his wife was not clear and I could hardly ask. A young girl, around five years old, appeared behind her. She looked like her mother – her long, flaxen hair, tied in a ponytail, staring up at us with bold curiosity.

"This is Georgina," said Carl, conversationally, "she's just started nursery school. She's always lived in London. It's been a shock for her, moving up North, hasn't it, sweetie?" He put his hand on her head and she leaned against him, staring at us, sucking her thumb. "But we've fixed her up in a nursery school, enrolled her in a dance school for talented kids. She's got a great future ahead of her. You're going to be a star, aren't you, honeybunch?"

"Yes, Pappa," she said.

I felt a pang of disappointment. They were an unlikely couple but a couple they obviously were.

"I'm going to be an actress," she confided, "Or a model. My

mamma was a model." She pointed to a photograph, framed on the wall, of a younger Patsy, posed Vargas girl-style, in white shorts, striped off-the-shoulder matelot's sweater and sailor's hat, looking cute and sexy.

The kitchen area was in the corner of the room and while Patsy busied herself with our refreshment, Carl made more small talk about the little girl – her ambitions and achievements, the auditions she had attended. By the time coffee was served, I feared there was a real danger of the Wunderkind breaking into a song from the musical, Annie.

Patsy intervened, "Oh, do stop, Carl. You mustn't encourage her to be the centre of attention all the time."

Nathan was, by now, trying to conceal his impatience. Mr. Fisher announced that he would bring in the picture. He reappeared with it in his hands face down. With an extravagant gesture, he turned it over for us to see. I looked at Nathan and Nathan looked at me. We had to smile. I had come all the way from London to see a painting I knew so well.

It was *Shops and People in Salford* – the painting Mr. Lowry had painted for the TV interview. I had not seen it for many years and I felt as though I was being reunited with an old friend. It was even more impressive than I remembered it; the figures painted in such detail, and so colourful. Mr. Lowry's white sky and background where he had baked the canvas were immaculate. The passage of time had shown the old master to be the genius I had told him he was at the end of the programme.

I explained to my hosts my previous connection to the painting and congratulated them on their good fortune in owning such a wonderful picture.

"Why all the secrecy?" I asked.

Mr. Fisher and Patsy exchanged glances. Both started to speak at the same time. It was clearly a delicate question and Patsy took over, "It's partly owned by the bank as security, and, at this stage, we wouldn't like them to know, that we're thinking of selling the picture."

It seemed a reasonable reply though it crossed my mind that, if the bank was holding the picture as security, why was it not physically holding the picture? How could they be showing it to us in their home? I set this thought aside as Nathan enquired about the provenance of the picture.

"Patsy inherited it."

"Hardly," she gave him a vexed look. "It belonged to my mother. My brother inherited it."

"Yeah, along with the million pound property, the estate and the holdings," said Carl. "Patsy didn't get a bean."

She quelled him with a cool glare. "My brother gave it to me. Suffice it to say, the provenance is impeccable."

We ummed and aahed, retired to confer privately with each other then feasted our eyes on it anew before, at last, Nathan delivered his verdict, "It's a superb painting you have. We know it well. It's worth a lot of money, but in our opinion, nothing like the figure you have in mind. As potential buyers at a lower figure, it is hardly in our interest to suggest a sale by auction, but after all's said and done, it's the only way to establish a value. How much, at maximum, it's worth to the highest bidder? If you think that you can get a million for it, then the auction rooms are your best bet."

Mr. Fisher said, "So you're passing on it?"

Nathan replied, "At the level you have in mind, yes. Let us think about it and perhaps we'll come back to you with a figure."

They didn't seem at all disappointed,

Mr. Fisher said, "This one's not negotiable. But, I'll be offering some other Lowry paintings at a lower price later in the year. I'll contact you then if you wish."

"That would be most interesting. Please do."

They exchanged addresses and phone numbers.

In the months that followed, I heard from Nathan that he had actually bought a Lowry from Carl Fisher called *Mill Gates*. He told me it was superb.

For my own part, I could not get the woman, Patsy Milford, out of my mind. I made some enquiries amongst other gallery owners and dealers but no one in the commercial art world seemed to know of her. And then it struck me that if she'd been a model it should be possible to find out more about her through the media route.

I rang Jenny Harding and arranged to meet her for lunch. She had access to the BBC archives and seemed to spend her life in the newspaper library at Colindale. "I don't know what the magazine was." I told her, "Maybe Vogue or Vanity Fair, top of the market stuff would be my guess. Something classy."

"Uhuh, Patsy Milford," said Jenny thoughtfully, sucking on the plastic device the Doctor had given her to help with the withdrawal pangs. It was shaped like a cigarette but a lot more hygienic. She had given up smoking two years before but showed no sign of ever giving up this plastic dummy. "Think I can save you a bit of work there. I used to know Patsy. We went to the same school."

I stared at her in astonishment.

"Yes," Jenny went on, "She's an old Rodeanian. "

"You went to Roedean?" If possible, this information astonished me even further – Jenny's speech was peppered with glottal stops and, if anyone had asked me, I would have guessed that she hailed from the Thames Estuary.

"Yuh. She was a few years ahead of me. Stunning looking girl with a good brain. Everyone expected her to go up to Oxford and read chemistry. She went off the rails got pregnant. It was all hushed up and she left under a cloud. Next thing, her old man's brought her a flat in Chelsea and she's flashing her assets on Page Three of the Sun for the world to see. Didn't go down well with the folks, or so I heard."

I was taken aback. It was hard to reconcile this information with the woman I had met.

A few days later, a large bundle of press clippings landed on my mat, courtesy of Jenny. It felt a little voyeuristic, ungallant even, to be flicking through them. There was nothing to be learned from them – other than the fact that she had a fantastic body, an angelic face.

At that point, I resolved to stop thinking about the enigmatic woman for, as I told myself, I had the next year's exhibitions to schedule and she most certainly wasn't thinking about me.

Later, that summer, I did the usual round of the art school graduate shows in the hope of 'discovering' a genius of the future. As I walked through the warren of studios on an upper floor at St. Martin's in Southampton Row, some vast abstract canvases in swirling dayglo colours arrested my attention. They had a certain panache, were vaguely reminiscent of de Kooning. As I stood back to appreciate them, an eager, bright-eyed, young girl student in crop-top and jeans came over, began to explain the images. When I mentioned my gallery space, her eyes lit up. It was then, as she was hauling out her portfolio from behind the plans chest, that my eyes settled on a flier on the notice board behind her.

Even as the girl was fetching out her unframed drawings, gesturing to her row of large, misshapen ceramic pots that were decorated with tribal feathers and beads, I completely lost interest in her and, like someone in a dream, sleep-walked over to the poster.

It read:

Commodification. The Price of Everything and the Value of Nothing. Public Lecture at the Institute of Contemporary Arts. Patricia Milford Art Historian BA Hons Fine Art. Tickets £7.50 at the door.

My heart leapt in my chest. I had a strange, inexplicable, feeling of certainty that Patricia was the Patsy, though this made no sense – Patsy was an ex-Page Three girl, not an art historian.

On the appointed evening, I was late. People tushed and tutted as I squeezed past them in the darkened room, towards one of the few empty seats. Slides of Jackson Pollock drip paintings were being projected on the big screen. An authoritative female voice was speaking over them, "... but as the artist acquires fame, so the work acquires financial value and the consumer society appropriates his product, corrupting the artistic impulse..."

When the lights came up, I saw it was indeed Patsy. She had on dark glasses, which seemed a touch eccentric given the dim wattage in the hall. Perhaps she thought these added to her air of film star mystery. There was certainly something of the ice-cold Hitchcock blonde about her, with her pale lilac suit, matching stiletto shoes and severe chignon.

The lecture covered pretty much what might have been expected – Walter Benjamin, Marcel Duchamp, George Grosz, Andy Warhol up to the present day – Hans Haacke through to Saatchi. "In the mass media society," she was saying, "art is little more than investment capital. So this is the challenge for the artist in a world of media saturation – to seek out ways to subvert the market, to appropriate material from the dominant cultural ethos for its own ideological purposes..."

I smothered a yawn. It was all a bit dry and polemical for me. At the end, there was earnest applause and questions from the crowd of intense students who were gathered. I sensed that she was glad when the whole thing was over and they began to file out of the room. I made my way down to the lectern where Patsy was packing up her slides and notes.

"Thomas Glaser," I said, "We met a few months ago. I came to see you in Hartlepool. To look at the painting?"

For a split second, a look almost of fear, crossed her face and then she recovered, smiled with professional charm, "Are you interested in the issues of commodification in mass media, Mr Glaser?"

"Certainly am. I understand now why you quoted us a million pounds for *Shops and People in Salford*. You wanted to get the word out and force the market up?"

She nodded. "The would-be buyers who came to see it told other would-be buyers and it created a buzz. We knew full well we wouldn't get a million, but the word of mouth hoiked Lowry prices up another notch."

"What did you get for it in the end?"

"We didn't sell."

Then I understood. "That wasn't the object of the exercise?"

She smiled, enigmatically.

"And you consider that legitimate business practice?"

"It's a game, Mr. Glaser. It's no different from the stock market, advertising – no different from selling anything. Pushing up the price of a stock artificially stimulates demand from the investors."

"Some of us love the paintings for their own sake."

"You own a gallery, Mr Glaser, you're part of the system, not the solution." She zipped up her bag with finality.

"Yes," I said, hurriedly, I could see she was about to sweep off, "...and that's why I wanted to talk to you. We have a modest performance space in the gallery. I'm thinking of starting a lecture series... Are you down in London long? Do you have any time when we might talk about that?" Close to, I could see the discoloration of the porcelain skin around her eye, despite the shades.

She hesitated, scrutinised my face, and then said, "Oh, what the hell. I could do with a drink."

Now she sat opposite me in the moody cocktail bar, drinking her second Margherita. She was relaxed now, had taken off the sunglasses so that the bruise around her eye was quite noticeable, "When my daughter was born, my mother was so outraged – she wouldn't even see her, said I'd thrown my life away. Despite all that, I got brilliant exam results. They'd always wanted me to do chemistry, but I went to Ruskin on a Fine Art scholarship. After my father died, the money stopped. I did the glamour modelling to support myself. And that was the last straw for my mother. She completely washed her hands of me. She died six months after my father. And then I found she'd left the entire estate to my brother and his ghastly wife.... seven million pounds worth. My brother gave me the Lowry because...." she gave an ironic smile, "it didn't go with his wife's upholstery. I was so hurt by the family's attitude that I vowed to make a fortune on my own." She stopped mid-stream, "I don't know why I'm telling you this... I don't usually pour my heart out to a total stranger..."

"I hope I won't always be a total stranger," I said, "I'd like to be a friend."

She shook her head, "No, I don't think that would be possible.... Well, you've obviously guessed that this...." she pointed to the bruise "...was no accident. He has a short fuse."

I said, "Forgive me if I'm speaking out of turn and I know it's difficult when he's the father of your child but..."

"Carl's not Georgina's father," she said, quickly. "He's good with her. She likes him. But he's not her father."

"Then why do you put up with violence? Why don't you leave him?"

She struggled with this question for a moment, then, "It's difficult. I can't explain. We go back such a long way. He's a rough diamond but... Carl's been good to me, to us. He's kept a roof over our heads. The house in Hartlepool is his.... And there are other things tying us together. I couldn't possibly make anyone else understand."

I dropped her back at her hotel, watched her until she was safely into the lobby. She waved. She seemed a small, vulnerable figure. As I drove away, I wondered what hold the man, Carl Fisher, had over her. I supposed that this was something I would never know.

CHAPTER 37

May 1986. Sitting at the head of the conference table, Nathan said, "The current financial position is pretty dire. I've called this crisis meeting to give you all the information we have to hand."

Alan, the financial director, had prepared a document, showing how badly the figures had deteriorated in the current year and handed it around the table to the other co-directors. He began, "The figures speak for themselves, but I need to inform the board, that VAT has not been paid for two quarters and the amount owing is one hundred and sixty five thousand pounds. I've had the Final Notice for ten days and if not paid very soon, we can expect the closure routine, which will give us the worst of all worlds. I assess that we have a week at the most." His face was grim. A large man with thick greying hair and designer stubble to match, he was brilliant at figures and had saved many a situation in the past. He had been handsomely rewarded with a directorship and a complimentary share allocation. But today he had no solutions to offer.

Nathan looked to Roy, who was both his accountant and a family friend. At a private meeting, they had considered the options and mapped out a game plan. Roy spoke for him. "Clearly we don't have time on our side. There are only two options at our disposal. Looking at the figures, I have to say that liquidation must be my best advice..."

Nathan shuddered at the mention of the word.

"...Cut your losses and run." continued Roy, "Bad luck for VAT and creditors, but no way should you throw good money after bad..."

Nathan shook his head. Fifty years had passed since his parents' triumphant opening of Grunfeld's knitting plant in Manchester. He could hardly believe that he was now fighting for its survival.

"There must be an alternative..."

"The alternative," said Roy, "is to inject five hundred thousand pounds, and hope that, given time, the stock will reduce and sales improve." He looked sharply at Nathan, "Playing Devil's advocate, what could you tell me that will encourage the bank, your colleagues and me, to recommend any course other than liquidation?"

Nathan replied, "We have an answer. A new label, different merchandise, more youthful styles, an extended clientele. Helen, perhaps you'd care to elaborate."

Helen stood up. Helen Catchpole, the woman he had so loved in his youth, had come back into his life the previous year. Following the death of his mother, they had met by chance and arranged to have dinner together, just for old times sake. She had matured but still had the same good looks and exuberant personality.

Twice widowed herself, Helen was a free agent. She had indicated that she would be happy to rekindle their love affair. Although tempted, Nathan had made it clear that he would always be faithful to Hannah. This had not stopped her from accepting his offer to join the company. He had never forgotten the speed and skill with which she had created a new design, when stopped in her tracks by his mother. Nathan had appointed her to design a new range for the younger market. And here she was now, he thought, anxious to repay his confidence by working day and night in getting the new range into the market place.

She cleared her throat, ready to address the board for the first time. "I've been engaged to produce a new range which we're calling 'Young Elite.' The first range went out last year with encouraging results. I think you opened nearly one hundred accounts, John?" She turned to John, the sales manager who corrected her, "One hundred and seven, to be exact."

Helen continued, "And we achieved sales that first season of a quarter of a million pounds. The goods were well delivered and we are getting very encouraging feedback. I am now preparing the second range. I'm optimistic that we will take twice as many orders. That means the first year's turnover could reach three quarters of a million, which we all think is a brilliant result for year one. I'm really impressed with the way in which John and his team have done so well."

John interrupted, "It's not me. It's Helen's merchandise which is brilliant. It walks off the shelves. It sells itself."

Helen smiled, looked round at the other directors, "Don't you think it's worth giving it a proper trial. We've started something that could revolutionize the whole company. This could really take off."

The co-directors looked at each other. Roy summed up, " Well, you've certainly given us a 'hope' factor. Whether there is sufficient hope to justify a half million investment is another matter..."

"We can do it," interjected Helen. "We'll turn hope into reality, I promise you."

Roy continued, "If you so decide, we would issue new share capital and I am authorized to suggest, that John and Alan, by virtue of their free share allocation, would receive a two for one issue of new shares, giving them ten percent of the new company for 25k each. Nathan would inject 450k to give him eighty percent."

Alan made a note of the proposal on his pad, but he didn't look too thrilled with the plan. Helen, on the other hand, listening carefully to all that was being said, was enthusiastic, "I think that's a great idea," she said, "Would you grant me the same option?"

Nathan had been glum throughout Roy's speech. He stared across at her. A broad smile crossed his face. "Nothing would give me greater pleasure than for you to have the same option as the others."

Alan and John gave little indication of similar enthusiasm. Roy summed up, "We seem to have reached some measure of agreement. If Nathan can raise four hundred and twenty-five thousand and the three Directors twenty-five thousand each, then we'll all pull together and give it our best shot. I suggest that we meet again in seven days time. I urge you all to think long and hard about your response."

Nathan did think it through long and hard. He was thinking that if he had to raise that amount of money, he would have to sell his beloved Lowrys. He did not think that his co-directors would come up with any contribution. Only Helen, loyal, adorable Helen.

Should he call in the receivers? He was a proud man. How could he grovel at creditors' meetings? And what would his community think of him, of the immensely respectable Nathan Grunfeld with a bankrupt company, whose loyal employees would all be out of a job?

Yet, what were the options? Put in more money? Alan claimed that it would do no more than 'buy time'. It was money down a bottomless pit. And would it buy enough time to benefit from the new label? Should he reduce the operation and sack half the staff? Probably too little and too late to have an impact.

Whenever there was a crisis in his life, Nathan would settle in his favourite armchair, fill a pipe and gaze at his beloved paintings, as though the little figures, scurrying about their business, could find a solution to his problem. He cleared the smoke that clouded his vision. He focussed on his favourite, '*Going to Work.*'

This was the Northern way of life that he cherished, and in the paintings he saw the industrial scene that he was fighting to preserve. How could he possibly sack his staff? They were his family and he was loyal to his family. All his life he had been a fighter, not a quitter. This, he thought, was not the time to become one. It was strange how studying the pictures made him feel calm.

That night he slept fitfully with the weight of these momentous matters. In the morning he rang Gavin Larkspur at Sotheby's and enquired whether he would visit his home in Hale, since he wished to dispose of some of his pieces. With such a coup in prospect for the next Auction, for which lots were closing within three days, Gavin did not delay.

He studied each painting with meticulous care. His magnifying glass enlarged every brushstroke. Finally he said, "Indeed, you have a magnificent collection. It would be an honour to handle them in our rooms, but tell me a little about the provenance of '*Mill Gates*....'

REAL ART

CHAPTER 38

Carl Fisher was on an ego trip. He stood naked in front of a full length mirror. What he saw was pleasing to the eye, certainly to his. He flexed his muscles. After regular work at the gym, the body responded to his satisfaction. He turned sideways for a profile view with equal gratification. He squeezed some hair gel into the palm of his hand and gently rubbed it into his scalp, disturbing the blond hair, with the darker roots – that had been so carefully arranged. He brushed, combed and patted it with care and soon achieved the look he sought to create. He moved his face closer to the mirror to trim his eight- day growth. Not too much though, since he liked to retain the unshaven look. He cut a few offending hairs from his nostrils. Finally a lotion, with powerful aroma on his face and body, well massaged into the working areas of his six-foot frame. He smiled at the mirror in approval. His teeth were not his best feature. Stained yellow by lack of care in his youth, he had the added misfortune of a gap upper front, where a tooth had been taken out in a fight. Now that he was in funds, he had meant to get it fixed and would do so soon.

Watching himself in the mirror as he dressed, he put on his favourite brown shirt with black tie and smart pinstripe suit. For final touch, he bound a cloth bearing the swastika insignia of the neo-Nazi party around his arm. He longed for the day when it would no longer be necessary to hide his affiliation beneath his jacket. Having completed his formal attire, he slipped his heavily padded trousers over his suit and zipped up the matching jacket, picked up his helmet and boots and with a final glance in the mirror for approval, made his way downstairs.

He liked his bike to be impeccable. Even though he was going to ride the 100-mile journey in darkness, he could not resist dusting the chrome engine casing, the drag bars and 21-inch front wheel before setting off. He caressed the handlebars and controls with affection.

Satisfied that his machine was beyond scrutiny, he wheeled it out of the garage and on to the road. He sat astride, put his helmet in position and with the lightest flick of his leg got an immediate response as his bike roared into action. Cruising down the motorway at 90mph, swerving from lane to lane was the source of great happiness to him. He felt at one with the machine. It answered his every call. He could forget the engine and felt like gliding free-wheel, the tilt of his body going first left, then right following the contour of the road.

When he reached his destination, he parked in the grounds, removed his leathers and helmet, gave his hair some attention, straightened his tie and looked the perfect businessman ready to negotiate a deal. He released the package from the back of his bike, took it with him and rang the doorbell. Nathan opened the door and shook his hand, saying, "Hello, Mr. Fisher. I've been waiting for you... do come in. I see you've brought the pictures."

Carl replied, "I'm sure your gonna like 'em..." He untied the package and placed the two canvasses, tilted face down by the side of the sofa. He thought he would get more impact by revealing each one separately.

"You were pleased with the last one?" asked Carl.

"I've asked you back," replied Nathan, guardedly. "let's see what you've got today."

Carl picked up the first canvas, flipped it face up and handed it to his client for examination.

It was a typical L.S. Lowry painting called '*Street Scene*'. It showed tall angular buildings, leading to a factory complex, with large figures in the foreground.

Nathan looked at it from all angles, up close, from afar and finally placed it on the mantelpiece to consider its merits. He seemed to show undue interest in the white skyline, having noted that the back of the canvas was without stickers. Carl broke the silence.

"Lovely 'in't it?"

165

"And the provenance?"

"Same as the last one. My friend is a keen collector and it comes from his collection."

"And the price?"

"Because there 'ain't no dealer involved, I can offer it to you for twenty five thousand pounds."

Nathan took the canvas off the mantelpiece and studied it again, closely. He said in a low offbeat voice, "Your friend, the keen collector, is perhaps something of an artist himself?"

"I dunno what'ya mean..."

"What I mean, Mr. Fisher is that this picture is clearly a copy, a good copy – as is the one you sold me four months ago."

"No, mate. Straight up. My friend's a genuine collector. I'm sure he wouldn't give me no copy."

Nathan was by now shaking with emotion, belying his cool exterior. He spoke slowly but calmly, still studying the painting. "The painting I bought from you four months ago was sold to me as an original Lowry, called 'Mill Gates'. I have irrefutable evidence it's a forgery."

Carl shook his head, "Nah, mate, you're wrong. This is the genuine article. I got papers to prove it. I'd stake me life on it."

"Sotheby's think otherwise. Would you like to read their report?"

"If Sotheby's say it's a copy, they're wrong, man," he repeated, beginning to break out in sweat. "I don't know what you're on about..."

"I think you do. The report states, among other things, that this canvas was painted within the last two years. L.S. Lowry died ten years ago. There can be no doubt whatsoever, that it's a forgery."

Carl's corner was getting smaller. He shrugged his shoulders, "It's a loada rubbish but I'll speak to me friend."

"I'm sure you will.... Tell him I want immediate refund of the twenty thousand pounds I paid for it."

"He won't do that. No way. Anyway, he's out of the country. I don't know how to contact him right now...."

Nathan moved towards the phone and lifted the receiver. "In that case, we'll see what the Police have to say..."

Carl had to make a split decision. Either pick up the pictures and run or resort to violence. Pushing Nathan away from the phone with far more force than necessary, he wrenched the cord out of the wall.

Nathan fell heavily to the floor, hitting his head on the corner of the table. He lay there for a moment, dazed, rubbing his head. Then stumbled to his feet, cast around for a weapon. He picked up a chair, swung it through the air and, with all his strength, whacked Carl round the head with it.

Reeling from the blow, Carl pulled his flick knife from his jacket and crouching forward commando-style, beckoned him, "Come on, yer' fuckin' Jewish bastard." A trickle of blood was running down the side of his face. Nathan was swinging the chair from side to side, hoping to score another hit. They stalked each other across the room, knife versus chair.

Nathan, near exhaustion, threw the chair at his assailant with all his remaining strength. It hit Carl squarely, knocking him back. Infuriated, Carl lunged forward pointing the knife at Nathan, who was defenceless against him. Carl pulled Nathan towards him and they stood eye to eye.

At that moment, Carl plunged the knife with all his force into Nathan's chest.

Nathan screamed.

Carl pulled the knife out.

Still staring at Carl, Nathan's hand went to his heart. He looked down. The blood was spurting, pumping from the mortal wound, spreading out until, before his eyes, his shirt became a soaking mess of red. White with shock, he staggered and fell to the ground. As the life-blood seeped out of him, his eyes glazed over and he drifted into unconsciousness.

Carl, sweating profusely and covered in blood, closed the flick-knife and grabbed the two canvasses.

The room was in chaos. He wanted to exit as quickly as possible but first removed the swastika insignia from his arm, and using it to wipe the fingerprints from all items he remembered touching.

Finally he dropped the armband onto the body of the dying man.

CHAPTER 39

I could hardly believe the news when I read about it. Nathan dead. Murdered – how was such a thing possible? The Jewish Chronicle had made it their headline story with a full centre page obituary. I stared at the photograph of Nathan framed heavily in black.

Much was made of his activity at the Nüremberg trial and there was even reference to his meeting with Hermann Göring. This seemed to be of special interest, since the Police had revealed that a swastika armband was found near the body. It fuelled the flames of suspicion that the murder may have been the work of a revenge hit squad.

I telephoned Hannah at once. She was in such shock, she could hardly speak. I managed to extract details of the Shiva and told her I would be there to pay my respects.

The Police came to the gallery, spent hours with me. They were interviewing friends, business colleagues and family to create a profile. Who could have wanted Nathan dead? They could find no motive from those they interrogated. They worked in liaison with Interpol and the German Police to study Nazi cells that were operating under cover, still in allegiance to their dead Führer.

Jenny agreed to come with me for the Shiva. She was interested to see Nathan's collection even though she had never met him, and I promised her some lighter moments at the Piccadilly Hotel.

We reached the house in Hale by late afternoon. The front drive-way was crammed with cars, parked nose to tail. There must have been two hundred people present. They were packed shoulder to shoulder in the hall leading to the living rooms and study. The atmosphere was subdued. Friends embraced. Strangers spoke to one another.

Poor Hannah, wearing a loose-fitting long black gown, was surrounded by well-wishers, paying their respects. She had matured into an elegant woman, but looked very pale with reddened eyes.

The Rabbi spoke prayers, joined by the congregation when appropriate. They knew the procedures well enough. There were audible sobs during his eulogy, "Surrounded as we are by these beautiful pictures of the North, I am reminded that Nathan once told me that he would like nothing better than to be a man in the crowd, just like one of Lowry's figures, going to work with the masses and staying anonymous. Instead, he became a Captain of Industry, taking over the family business of Grunfelds, started by his late parents. To this he dedicated his entire life, making it one of the most successful and prosperous companies in the world of fashion..."

At this point, Alan and John, who had joined the mourners to pay their respects, could not refrain from exchanging glances.

Helen was standing with Roy, staring straight ahead. She was dry eyed but had a look of real anguish on her face. I thought how hard it must be for her to be here, mourning Nathan, in the role of disinterested spectator when she had once been his passionate lover and indeed, unbeknown to Hannah, his intended wife.

The Rabbi continued, "Above all, he was a fine human being and there can be no greater honour to him than to see so many of his friends here tonight. I once asked him what he would have done, had he not become an industrialist. Characteristically, he replied without hesitation, '*Play centre forward for Manchester United*'" There was laughter, which released the tension amidst the sadness and gravity of the occasion.

As we filed out of the room with Alan and John, Alan said, "Whoever did it, chose his moment well. I think he would have been in for a rough ride, poor bastard."

"How d'you mean?" I asked.

"Well, I certainly wouldn't have put money in. Would you, John?"

He was undecided. "I was thinking I might, if you had,"

Alan said. "Well, it's a different ball game now."

John lowered his voice, "You mean you'd do a deal with the receiver?"

I was a little shocked to hear them spell out their intentions quite so soon after the funeral, but I saw that fate had played into their hands and delivered the opportunity of a magnificent prize, which would never have been theirs, had Nathan lived.

Grimly, Alan concluded, "We could take over the business for next to nothing, liquidate and start again with a clean slate. That's a scheme worth going for, I can tell you."

When the mourners had all but departed, Jenny and I went back into the main room to pay our respects to Hannah. She was standing with Helen and Roy. We embraced her each in turn.

"So pointless," she repeated for the second time. "And for what? It's so terrible not to know who did this wicked thing and why."

I replied, "Nathan was my closest friend. We spent a precious year together at Nüremberg. He didn't have an enemy in the world. So I can't really swallow this revenge killing story."

She nodded, "Speak to any of his staff, to anyone in the community and they will all say, he was the kindest, most caring, considerate..." at this, she broke down again, "...man in the world..."

Helen put her arms around her and comforted her. I took her hand, "I'd very much like to stay in touch, Hannah. If I can help you in any way in the future, please call me. I'll always be at your disposal." "Thank you. You're very kind, Thomas," she said.

On our way out, Jenny and I walked round the room, looking at the Lowrys. There were twelve in all. It was a rare occurrence to see so many gems assembled in one room. I recognised most from my previous viewing at the wedding. Even so, it was breath-taking to revisit. They seemed to have mellowed with age. *Going to Work*, An *Industrial Scene* and *Crime Lake* were the stars of the show. It was lovely to see again *Yachts at Lytham* and memories of the wedding, and Mr. Lowry's gift of that picture came flooding back. What a happy occasion that was. And what a contrast, this.

Of those I hadn't seen before, two were outstanding. One was a beautiful beach scene, a very happy typical Lowry seascape with lots of figures enjoying the sun and sea.

The other called *Mill Gates* worried me a little. It contained all the ingredients a collector would wish for – people of all sizes, the dogs, an archway through which were buildings with smoking chimneys, mills heavy with figures coming and going.

And yet... I examined it more closely. The colours were unusually bright. I focused on the white background. It was a smooth white texture, brighter than usual. The antique look was missing. This canvas had not been 'baked.' The picture was signed L. S. Lowry alright, but somehow it looked too flat and recent to be real.

I looked at the back to see if the familiar Lefevre sticker was there, which would have guaranteed its authenticity. It was bare, without any indication of its provenance. The title and date were written in crude capitals with a thick pen.

I pondered, what would Nathan be doing with a fake in his collection? To make up the numbers? To fill a space on the wall? Or had he bought it believing it to be authentic?

In the car, driving to the Piccadilly Hotel, where I had booked a room for the night, I said to Jenny, "One of his Lowrys is a copy."

"Really," Jenny responded without much interest, "Which one?"

"The one called *Mill Gates*."

"Who cares?" she was preoccupied with her own programme.

"I do," I replied, "he's only got eleven, not twelve. That makes it a dead heat."

CHAPTER 40

I always looked forward to receiving the catalogues for the 'Modern British' auctions, which arrived through my letterbox usually in May and November. I would turn the pages eagerly, waiting to fall upon the Lowrys that were coming up for sale. Mostly, they were left to the end of the book as star exhibits. So it was, with the latest Sotheby's catalogue, displaying a full colour page for each of the six Lowrys to come under the hammer.

When I turned the page of the third Lowry, I could hardly contain my excitement, to see illustrated a picture with which I had a strong personal relationship. It was *Shops and People in Salford*.

Memories flooded back. The meeting with the artist at his house, watching him physically paint this masterpiece. The way I had ended the interview came to mind, *'Mr. Lowry, I think you are a genius.'* Prophetic words.

Then I recalled seeing the painting in Hartlepool with Nathan. Carl Fisher and Patsy Milford claiming ownership and asking a million for it. What a ridiculous price tag that had been? Here it was estimated at two hundred to three hundred thousand – a little more realistic. I studied the small print and noticed 'By order of the Trustees.' This indicated to me that either the owner had died or that it secured a loan that had defaulted.

I thought it unlikely that Patsy or Carl Fisher had died. What an ill matched couple they had been, unlikely owners of that wonderful picture. It was over a year ago that Nathan and I had been there. Nathan had been dead ten months now. I spoke to Hannah quite often. She was still in deep mourning. The police had made no arrest. The murderer was still at large.

I went through my file, in which I kept a record of Lowrys I had seen, and found my notes with the address in Hartlepool. Assuming the couple was not dead, it must be that the Trustees were selling on their behalf for one reason or another. Not knowing preyed on my mind. Here was a picture, which, because of my association with it, I would desperately like to see hanging on my walls. As I tossed and turned in semi-sleep, I hatched the embryo of an idea. Why not take a trip to Hartlepool, breeze in and ask if I could help? Maybe the couple had financial problems, which an immediate cash injection could resolve. After all, they could withdraw the picture from auction at any time and if I were to be their 'white knight' they could save themselves ten per cent commission plus VAT. Quite a saving on a picture of that price or maybe the Trustees, if I could find out who they were, might be similarly inclined.

In the cold light of day, I dismissed the idea. Yet, two to three days on, I still found myself subconsciously calculating how I could raise a quarter of a million. I could not get it out of my mind and, fired by the fact that I had a blank diary for the following week, I made the decision.

I arrived at around seven in the evening. The front door was opened by Georgina. She looked very like her mother. Long, blonde hair hanging loose about her shoulders and a fringe over her forehead. Wearing jeans and a denim top that left her midriff uncovered, she looked a prototype model-to-be. "What do you want?" she demanded.

"Could I have a word with your Mum and Dad?"

She opened the door wider. "Come in. I'll go get Mum."

I followed her into the front room. She went out into another room and I heard her leave the house by the back door, which she slammed behind her, leaving me to get my bearings. And then I noticed the painting on the wall. I felt my heart lurch in my chest and begin to pump faster.

The last time I had seen the picture, was on Nathan's wall. It was 'Mill Gates', one of Lowry's finest, in immaculate oil and signed clearly, L.S. Lowry. It was perfect to the eye, brilliant in its execution. Only an expert would detect the flat white background, as tell-tale. My brain was in overdrive. Was this the same picture I had seen on Nathan's wall, or another copy? Nathan's, of course, was elaborately framed, whilst this one was just the canvas.

No sign of Georgina or her mother, so instinctively, I turned it over to see if there were any stickers on the back. It was quite plain.

It was yet another copy. I needed time to think. What should I say to Patsy when she finally arrived? Should I tell her my conclusions?

I wandered over to the sideboard. On it there were some Polaroid snapshots. I thumbed through them. They were mostly of Georgina, some with her mother, but the one that stopped me in my tracks was another subject. It was Carl in full Nazi regalia. The peak cap, with its skull and crossbones insignia on it, black jacket with an iron cross on his left chest, with other decorations and jackboots. On his arm the black, white, red swastika symbol.

Even at this moment, I knew that, unintentionally, I had stumbled upon the pieces of the jigsaw that had eluded the Police for ten months. I slipped the incriminating photo into my jacket pocket. Of course, what I should have done next was to leave by the same front door through which I had arrived and head for the nearest Police Station. Instead, I went through the hallway and kitchen and out of the back door, by which Georgina had left the house to find her mother.

A few steps away there was an outhouse, which appeared to have been converted into a studio. Through the window, I could see Patsy pacing in agitation, talking animatedly on the phone. She looked very different – dishevelled and without makeup. Her blonde hair tied up in a casual knot. Wearing a well-worn painter's smock tied apron-style, she had taken on a persona not previously seen…one of 'gravitas,' at work in her studio.

I took it all in at a glance and understood. An easel with a half finished Lowry on it; another with a print, obviously the source material, covered with squared up tracing paper. Two palettes with a huge variety of colours on each, an array of brushes standing in turps; tubes of paint scattered everywhere, and – most incriminating of all – canvasses propped up against the wall. Lowrys. A regular production line of Lowry copies, quite enough to saturate the market.

Even at this point, having seen all I wanted to, I could have cut and run. I now had compelling evidence that these people were linked to Nathan's murder, but something drew me on. I had come a long way and wanted some questions answered.

I knocked on the door and entered. Georgina put her hand over her mouth and said, "Oh sorry Mum, I forgot to tell you. He was waiting for you in the house."

Patsy muttered into the phone then put down the receiver, tried to block my path, "I don't know what you want, but..." trying to push me out, "...this is a private studio. You have no right to be here. I'm warning you... Carl's on his way here right now..."

"I'm not frightened of Carl," I said.

In a brittle voice, laced with urgency, "Georgina, darling, go into the house and wait for Pappa."

I should have left then. Carl was a violent man, who had killed once and would not hesitate to kill again. Instead I said, "I've come here to talk to you about my friend. Nathan. You remember Nathan, the man who was here with me when I came last year?"

She seemed to relax, nodded.

"He was murdered. About ten months ago."

Either she was as brilliant an actress as she was an artist or she was genuinely horrified at this news; she covered her face in her hands and said a single word, "How?"

"He was stabbed to death," I said, "The murder weapon was never found, but the killer left behind a swastika armband."

I threw in this bit for gratuitous information so that, if she didn't know about the murder, she must surely by now have realized the identity of the killer. She was silent.

What her reply would have been will never be known, since at that moment Carl Fisher came into the studio. He had on a sleeveless t-shirt and shorts. His biceps were impressive, his skin heavily tattooed, his thighs massive, he was a hulk of a man. He must have come from physical exercise – he was sweating profusely, dabbing his face with the towel curled around his neck. He looked up at me and his face contorted. I had the impression of a snorting bull about to charge, "What the hell you doin' 'ere?" he demanded, "This is private property an' you're trespassin'."

"It's OK, Carl," said Patsy, "He's here about the picture."

He took no notice. As far as he was concerned, I had discovered their line of business and he didn't like it. He moved towards me, menacingly, grabbed the front of my shirt and pulling me towards him, said through clenched teeth, "You got no bleedin' right to be 'ere."

I pushed him away from me with all the strength I could muster.

Within a second, he was at my throat, throttling me. Patsy was shouting, "Stop, Carl, stop it. No violence."

My shirt tore as we disengaged and he fell away with it in his hand. I managed to break his hold. He landed a blow on my chin, which felled me. I lay on the floor, stunned. He was trying to pick me up off the floor to finish me off, but Patsy pushed herself between us. He pushed her away and renewed the heavy blows to my face and body. I got to my feet, reeling, dabbing my wounds with what remained of my shirt. I was breathing heavily. I gasped out, "I know you murdered Nathan Grunfeld. And the Police know it too. The Police are on their way here to arrest you."

"No. I don't believe it," Patsy cried out, "Say you had nothing to do with it, Carl. Tell me you don't know what he's talking about..."

But instead, berserk with rage, he began swinging punches at me. I fell to the ground again. Now, he was on top of me, his massive hands squeezing my windpipe. I felt the blood vessels bulging in my head as if they would burst. Choking, wheezing, desperate for breath... I had the heel of my hand hooked under his chin, trying to push his face upwards and away but I was ineffectual. Without breath, I was losing strength and power. With a supreme effort, I stretched, groped for the jar of turpentine that was just out of reach. As my hand closed round it, I jerked it forward, exploded the contents into my assailant's eyes.

Momentarily blinded, he let out a curse. His hands went to his eyes. He creased up, howling with pain.

Patsy took her advantage, picked up a plank of wood and hit him across the head with it, once, twice, three times until it splintered. He reeled and, still blind, staggered out of the room.

I stood with head bowed, breathing heavily, physically exhausted. Blood was pouring from my mouth and nose. There was a gaping cut down one side of my face. One eye was closing up.

Patsy was crying. The half-completed Lowry was on the floor ruined, the easel broken. The window smashed. Tubes of paint were scattered over the floor. We stood there, amidst the wreckage. Neither of us had the strength to speak.

Seconds later, the roar of a motorbike's engine being started, could be heard. Carl revved the throttle and sped off into the night.

CHAPTER 41

Carl headed for the open highway. While he was on the bike, no one could touch him. They were an indestructible team – him and his bike.

Twenty miles and no sign of the Police. That guy had obviously been bluffing, he thought.

Riding that straight stretch of road without exit points, Carl heard the helicopter before he saw it. At first, he wasn't unduly alarmed. But then it seemed to be hovering above him. He tried slowing down, then accelerating. It was still there.

Alarm turned to panic as the blue flashing lights of the Police roadblock loomed ahead, maybe four hundred yards away. He slowed down as he approached. Off the hard shoulder, there was a track. Could he make it through there? This called for precision riding, split second timing. But then two Police officers took his space and he saw they were carrying the Stinger net that they threw down to puncture tyres.

He swung the machine into a u-turn and accelerated in the opposite direction, sped away at maximum speed.

The helicopter was still tracking him but now there was an additional hazard. Two Police bikes were in hot pursuit. He squeezed his accelerator to maximum and clocked 122 mph. It was the fastest he had ever travelled. But they were still there, keeping pace. And so was the helicopter.

Suddenly, there was a bend in the road. He couldn't afford to slow down. The Police were too close. He took it at the same speed. The angle of the bike was alarming. His left knee was scraping the road. Whether this caused the crash or he simply lost control, will never be known.

The Police watched helplessly as the bike took three somersaults and then bounced and skidded some two hundred yards away from the point of impact.

CHAPTER 42

Inspector Bob Wilson, who was leading the Murder investigation, visited me on my second day in hospital and informed me that Carl Fisher had been killed. I was shocked at the news.

The nurse brought me a hand mirror. I hardly recognised myself. Both eyes were black and heavily swollen. There were stitch marks on forehead, chin and cheeks. It was a depressing sight. I felt immensely sorry for myself. Here I was, alone in Hartlepool Hospital. Where had I gone wrong? True, I had the superficial trappings of success – a home in Chelsea, a flourishing art gallery. But, right now, these were of little consolation. It was love and companionship I needed. I reflected on my life. Perhaps I had been too dismissive of affection when it had been offered, seeking perfection that did not exist. If so, I was surely paying the price now for my lack of commitment. I would have given anything for a soothing hand in mine, a worried wife at my bedside. With my face so battered, this prospect seemed ever more distant. The nurse gave me an infusion of morphine for the pain and I drifted into a troubled sleep.

I dreamed of the Kindertransport, of seeing my brother dragged away for the last time. My Mother was kissing me or was it Patsy involved in the dream somehow as either a nurse or an angel of death. It was difficult to disentangle the past from the present. And then I became aware of someone in the room, beside me; a cool hand mopping my brow. I muttered, "Patsy..."

She leaned forward, close enough that I could smell her perfume, and whispered, "Shush, you mustn't exert yourself. Just rest." I felt her hand close tenderly around my hand. I drifted back to sleep, feeling happier than I had felt in a long while...

When I opened my eyes, it was Hannah Grunfeld, matronly and overweight, leaning over me, pressing a poultice to my forehead, and now smiling, holding up a basket of fruit.

"Dear Tom," she said, planting a kiss on my cheek. She took both my hands and held them to her chest tightly, saying, "You've been so brave."

She sat at my bedside and began to rattle on – about how empty her life was without Nathan, how she was thinking about selling the house, which was too large for her anyway. "Not that I need to tell you about solitude, Thomas. You never married, did you? Perhaps we should get together. Two lonesomes on our ownsomes," she said lightly as a joke.

I didn't fancy myself in Nathan's shoes at all and simply closed my eyes and groaned a little, hoping that she might get the message. But no, when I opened them to check, she had taken her coat off, was settled back in the chair for the long haul, crocheting some sort of doily.

"And the Lowry's. Well, to tell you the truth," she was saying, "I never did love them like Nathan did. I'm thinking of selling them. What do I want with all those pictures?" She pulled a comic face, started singing, "*Matchstick men and matchstick cats and dogs...*"

This was torture to me. I tried to raise myself from my drugged torpor. I wanted to exclaim that Mr. Lowry had hated more than anything the accusation that he painted matchstick figures. He used to protest, '*I spent twelve years, drawing from life at art school.*'

She saw my movement, put down her crocheting, asked with a concerned face, "Is it water you want, Thomas?" began pouring water from the beaker down my gullet until I spluttered explosively, then sat down again and continued prattling. "You know, Thomas, I've never quite trusted Alan, or John. Even Roy, I'm not quite sure about. Nathan thought the world of them. But, well, the offer they made me on the factory, it was derisory. Rock-bottom. I was shocked. And then Helen said to me, '*You're the major shareholder now, Hannah. Don't let those sharks bamboozle you.*' I said, '*What choice do, I have, Helen?*' She said, '*Hannah, you get those account books and hand them over to me. You can sit beside me while I go through them and tell you exactly what's what...*' "

Through the morphine haze, I felt as though I was drifting. It was hard to focus on her face as it came in and out of focus.

"Apparently her spitfire pilot left her well provided for. And then, of course, she married his brother... turns out he was something of a magnate in the wire coil industry but tragedy struck him down young too. Anyway, Tom, I can see you're wilting... So to cut a long story short..."

God in heaven! Could anything cut the woman short?

"Me and Helen are going into partnership. I know it's what Nathan would want and you see," she gabbled on, "Nathan had his life well insured and I got a very good payment from this. So I thought, put it back into the business with some of Helen's money – she knows what it's all about and she'll make it work." She paused; I thought I had heard it all, but no. "John and Alan can put their two pennorth in if they want to, or Helen says she'll buy them out... She's got an answer for everything that one."

Her honest, innocent face beamed at me. "'Grunfeld and Catchpole,' that's what we're going to call it."

With a supreme effort, I roused myself to drowsily repeat, "Grunfeld and Catchpole. Yes, that certainly has a ring to it."

She was in the doorway when she remembered something else. "I was going to ask you Tom," she said, "Nathan told me you were writing his life story..."

I murmured, "Long time ago, Hannah. All just talk. We didn't really mean it."

She persisted, "Oh, but he did, Tom. He often talked about it. He saw it as something tangible he could leave to..." her voice broke up now, "future generations..."

It was the last thing I wanted to discuss. For, even in my feeble state, her words jarred my conscience.

I was discharged days later. The papers had got hold of the story and, as I walked painfully out into the street, the Paparazzi were there in force.

PAGE THREE STUNNER IN NAZI MURDER QUIZ ARRESTED FOR ART FRAUD was the headline in *The Sun*.

Reading the article, I found that the investigation into Nathan's death was now closed. The circumstantial evidence I had provided had since been corroborated by the forensic team. It seemed that the tyre marks found in Nathan's front garden after the murder corresponded to the remnants of Carl's motorbike tyres.

"How's Miss Milton taking it?" I asked Inspector Wilson, when he rang.

I learnt that she was on remand, facing charges of fraud and forgery. Her solicitor was seeking bail but, apparently, she had been unable to provide sureties of a hundred thousand pounds. She was anticipating the imminent sale of a painting at auction, which would provide the necessary funding.

The title was *Shops and People in Salford*.

CHAPTER 43

"Lot 67." A buzz went around the auction room, as Shops and People in Salford was placed on the easel. It looked sensational from afar, quite the most important picture in the sale. The guide price was two to three hundred thousand. Three hundred thousand was my upper limit. The staff on the telephones were all on stand-by, waiting to take bids from outside the room.

I turned to Matthew Jackman who was sitting beside me, "How much d'you think it will make?" His gallery on Knightsbridge had handled most recent Lowry transactions. His clients numbered many showbiz personalities and politicians, who were eager buyers in a still rising market.

"I'll tell you something," he murmured, "at least four of my clients, to my knowledge, were offered the picture before the auction for one million pounds direct from the owner."

I interrupted, "You can add me to that list."

"They'll think they have a bargain if they get it for half that figure."

My heart sank at this. Maybe, I was wasting my time. Perhaps Patsy's long-term strategy to artificially boost the price was about to pay off. It would take the picture right out of my range.

But, just as Gavin Larkspur, the auctioneer, was about to commence the bidding, one of his colleagues appeared on the podium, holding a sheet of paper in his hand. There followed an uneasy silence, whilst he read it. He made a phone call, had a further conversation with the official and finally declared, "Ladies and Gentlemen, I'm very sorry for the delay, Lot 67 has been with-drawn for legal reasons. On to Lot 68…"

I was disappointed in the extreme. I turned to Mr Jackman for explanation but he shook his head, mystified. I stayed in my seat for the two remaining Lowrys, which terminated the auction. Then limped to the podium to see if I could find out why it had been with-drawn.

Gavin wouldn't say, but I hung around a little longer and over-heard a conversation between two officials. It appeared that the owner had procured a bank loan, using the picture as security. When the identical picture had appeared in the Sotheby's catalogue for auction, the bank had looked more closely at the item in their vaults. It hadn't taken them long to establish that they were holding a fake. With only three days to go before the auction of the genuine article, the bank had moved swiftly to obtain an injunction against their client, claiming ownership of the original and blocking its sale.

The consensus of opinion was that this legal action could take many months to unfold. It would indeed be unwise to forecast whether or when a new date of sale could be arranged.

I thought of poor, clever Patsy languishing in jail – it hadn't been too clever to raise a loan against a fake, for now she was unable to raise bail money against the original. Half a million had just slipped out of her grasp.

CHAPTER 44

I felt claustrophobic as the doors of H.M. Holloway prison closed behind me. I had to register, fill in a form, was searched and finally gained admission.

I was shown to the visitors' room on the first floor. A large, brightly lit room with no windows and a flat roof. There was a stale, airless stench, which I tried to filter out by breathing through my mouth. I noticed a snack bar at one end, a few people waiting to be served.

Some parties were already seated at tables engrossed in conversation. Children were running about, using the room as a playground.

Patsy duly arrived via a door at the far end, escorted by a prison officer. As she was on remand, she was allowed to wear her own clothing and appeared in jeans, sweater and jacket. She looked pale, but elegant, as ever, and in control. "It's very nice of you to come and see me," she said, "How are you feeling now?"

"As if I've been hit by a truck."

We sat at one of the tables, which I noticed was screwed to the ground. H. M. Prisons were taking no chances. The two warders watched each table closely, one standing by the far door, the other wandering amongst the tables, watching each group from a discreet distance.

"I'm so sorry about all that happened," she said, "Carl was a violent man but I never dreamed he was capable of murder."

"So you didn't know at the time that he'd murdered my friend, Nathan?"

She shook her head, indignantly, "Of course I didn't. If I'd known that, I'd have gone straight to the Police. I was horrified when I heard... Of course, I should have left him long before."

"Why didn't you?"

184

"The relationship was over but whenever I talked of leaving, he'd threaten to expose my part in the operation. Carl couldn't operate without me. He was the front man, taking the risks but I was the brains."

"So you knew that your copies were being sold as originals?" I persisted.

"Of course."

"And you didn't think there was anything... wrong... in that?"

"Wrong?" She repeated, "What a curiously old-fashioned man you are, Thomas."

It was the first time she had used my name and I liked the sound of it in her mouth as those fathomless blue eyes continued to mock me gently, "What do you mean by 'wrong'?" she queried, "What was done to your friend, Nathan, was wrong. Violence, destruction, hurting other people, that's wrong. But how could it hurt anyone for me to exactly reproduce a visually stunning picture so that it can give pleasure to more than one person?"

"It hurts the buyer," I retorted, "It means he's paying a price far in excess of what the painting's actually worth."

"And what is a painting worth? Who sets the price and decides the value? The dealers? The critics and the investment bankers? Who's to say that, if the copy's capable of giving the same visual pleasure, of evoking the same emotions in the viewer, as the original, that it isn't worth as much?"

I snorted, "I'm sure Mr. Lowry would have something to say about that..."

"I doubt it. Lowry despised most of the critics and dealers. He played tricks on them; he liked to see how far they would go to make a profit out of him. He was popular with real people and that made the critics look down on him. Maybe it was a class thing. They called him "a half-baked amateur... primitive... inept ... repetitive ... stuck in a rut..." But, once he died, they knew he was a gilt-edged stock and the investors' scramble started. Now we have a multi-million pound Lowry industry – a million miles away from the man, his intentions and his art. Do you think that what I do – paying homage to his skill – is more 'wrong' than those who just want to use his work as bullion in a bank – as a bulwark against inflation?"

Her argument interested me, "So you see yourself as a guerrilla, whose aim is to destabilise the market?"

"I see myself as an activist, a defender of true artistic values with a mission to subvert the immoral investment market that the art world has become."

"Yet simultaneously profiting from the same mega-bucks as the corrupt art world you're attacking? Good move, comrade."

She smiled, seemed not at all offended, "The wheel of irony never ceases to revolve. In fact, my stance on this issue could be viewed as a conceptual art work itself."

"You might try that as a defence, although your average jury could find it a touch abstruse."

"I paint a picture. Someone likes it enough to buy, and pays a price. It's as simple as that. Caveat emptor. 'Let the buyer beware'."

"Try telling that to your bank. The way they see it, the original gives you a 'get out of jail free' card. The fake entitles you to an extended stay at Her Majesty's Pleasure."

She made a face, "My solicitor's trying to get me bail. We have a few problems."

"Who's looking after Georgina?" I asked to change the subject.

Her face clouded at the reminder. "She's living in the mansion in Godalming, where I grew up. With my brother and his dreadful wife, no doubt inculcating her with their gruesome, bourgeois values."

"She'll be OK," I made a clumsy attempt to comfort her, "The main thing is for you to get out of here as soon as you can. Look, as I understand it, your bank has just realised that they're holding a copy and they've taken out an injunction to stop you from selling the original."

"How do you know that?" she asked.

"I'm trying to buy the original, remember," I said, "so I make it my business to know. If there's a fake sitting at the bank, it's very relevant. May I ask how much you owe the bank?"

"Twenty k plus interest."

"Sotheby's seem to think it could take a long time before the injunction was lifted."

"Really? You know more than I do."

"I also know that you need a hundred thousand bail to get out of this hell-hole." I felt I had made all the right moves. All that was left was for me to spell out my proposal. "Patsy, *Shops and People in Salford* is of great sentimental value to me. I was with Mr. Lowry when he painted it. I've travelled across the country twice to see it, nearly getting myself killed in the process. I think I've proved that it's not a matter of investment with me. Perhaps, I can solve your problem, and you mine."

She arched one perfect eyebrow, "I'm listening."

"My solicitor's of the opinion that a third party could intervene here and pay off the Bank to get the injunction lifted. At the same time there must be an offer to pay their legal fees if they agree to waive the writ and close their legal process."

"You'd be prepared to do that?"

"Obviously, only if I secure the picture – and I do mean the original." I began to disclose the plan that I had evolved over many a sleepless night, "Sotheby's would probably require some form of compensation for losing the sale after all the publicity. My solicitors would have to negotiate on your behalf. I would suggest maybe – twenty grand. I would agree to pay all expenses that I have described to you, which could total 60k, and pay you 200k for the picture." I paused to let the figure sink in, "It's a very fair offer." She was silent. I went on,

"Any sane person would respond by throwing their arms around me, crying, 'There really is a Santa. I accept'."

"Not my style, Thomas," she said with a curl of her beautiful lip.

The warder, who had been patrolling the tables nearby, looked at his watch and announced, "Five minutes ter go. Time ter wind up. Say yer goodbyes."

I gave her my card and rose to leave. We shook hands and I wished her luck. I thought, 'See you in three years.' I was halfway to the door when she called me back.

"Thomas? Make it two hundred and ten."

I recalled Mr. Jackman's remark that there were at least four buyers likely to bid five hundred thousand, and that my own limit was to be three hundred thousand.

"Two hundred and ten, if you throw your copy in with it."

She gave a smile of quiet satisfaction; "I'll talk it through with my solicitor."

As I walked to the door, the children in the room were clinging to their mothers and crying. It must have been beyond their understanding why their relative could not come home with them. My heart went out to these women whom fate had brought here. For what kind of 'criminals' were they? Just fine-defaulters, shoplifters, streetwalkers... Half an hour in H. M. Prison Holloway as a visitor was bad enough. To be holed up within those forbidding walls for any longer would be a dismal plight indeed.

As I breathed the air of Brixton, I thought my mission had been a success. I was relieved to leave that depressing, austere building a free man.

CHAPTER 45

The next time I saw Patsy was in court. She stood in the dock, flanked by a prison warder. Her hands were demurely folded in front of her. She looked angelic, dressed with a simplicity that spoke for her innocence. She wore a pale blue classic twin-set with a dark pencil skirt. An unobtrusive gold chain around her neck. Her hair had grown since I last saw her; it hung loosely around her shoulders. The only make-up I could detect was about her eyes. She had elected to present herself in a very natural, 'girl-next-door' way, and I found the image immensely appealing.

The moment I entered the courtroom, our eyes met. She smiled at me, made no effort to conceal her gratitude that I had come to give evidence in her favour.

"The late Carl Fisher, and he only, is guilty of these offences," said the defending barrister, Mr. Richard Baskin. "My client is an artist pure and simple. She paints for pleasure. She was trained to paint and if it pleases her to make a transcription of an Old Master or a modern work of art, it is her privilege to do so. If others choose to take advantage of her undoubted skills, then so be it. My client played no part whatsoever in the activities of which she stands accused."

David Delgado, Counsel for the prosecution begged to differ, pointing out that signing the artist's name on each picture, constituted an act of forgery.

"Not if the painting is for home consumption," Mr. Baskin was quick to interject.

But he found himself on less safe ground, when the prosecution summoned Mr. David Smythe, Bank Manager at Hartlepool. He stated, under oath, that Patsy was indeed his former client, who had negotiated a twenty thousand pound loan, secured by an original Lowry oil painting, which was now shown to be a worthless copy.

He was quick to stress in his defence, that he had been shown the original, of that he was quite certain, and it was his contention that it had been switched to the excellent copy that had been delivered to the Bank. Documentation was produced which bore Patsy's signature to show that she was both guarantor and account holder.

Mr. Baskin was on his feet again. He was quick to establish that Mr. Fisher was present at that interview with the Bank and that it was Mr. Fisher who had delivered the picture. "...Therefore," he concluded, "It would be quite reasonable to assume that his client's good name was being used to the benefit of Mr. Fisher's fraudulent intent."

The defence called its first witness. I swore to 'tell the truth, the whole truth, and nothing but the truth.' Mr. Baskin led me through an account of our first meeting, underlining heavily that it was Mr. Fisher who had telephoned me originally and that it was he who had conducted the abortive negotiation. Patsy had not been involved at all, other than to prepare refreshments.

"Now would you be so kind as to tell Milord and the jury, exactly what took place in the late afternoon of August the 12th at the house in Hartlepool, home of the defendant." Mr. Baskin was relying heavily on my statement to swing the proceedings in his favour. I started nervously, explaining the reason for my second visit and covered every detail leading up to Carl's assault.

"There is no doubt in my mind at all, that Mr. Fisher would have killed me, had it not been for Ms Milford's intervention. He had me by the throat in a death lock. He was throttling me. She hit him repeatedly with a plank of wood. I've no doubt at all that she saved my life."

Mr. d'Elgado rose to his full height, well over six foot, and clutching the edges of his gown with both hands, he looked a confident and imposing adversary. "You a family man?" he asked.

"No," I said.

"I note with interest that you first met the accused in her home in Hartlepool some years before the assault took place."

I agreed.

"For the benefit of Milord and the Jury, can you enlarge on what took place on that day?"

"It was just a meeting between strangers, who had travelled a long way to see a painting.

Mr. d'Elgado pursued his point, "Were you alone with Ms Milford?"

I cast my mind back, trying to remember.

"Mr. Fisher greeted us at the door; then she arrived; she made refreshments, while we made small talk until the picture was produced."

"I see," the barrister said nonchalantly, "and did he go out of the room to fetch the picture?"

I replied quickly, "If he did, it was only for a matter of seconds."

"Were you in conversation with her, whilst he was out of the room?"

I wracked my brain, "I really cannot remember. If anything was said, it can have been no more than a few words."

"At the time you first met her, what was your impression of the accused?" he asked in full voice.

"I thought her a very attractive, educated lady."

Patsy threw me a radiant smile.

"And what was your opinion of Mr. Fisher?"

"I wondered what she could possibly have in common with him," I stated.

It was the answer Mr. d'Elgado was hoping to hear. With a smile on his face, he said, "I understand what you are trying to say. You thought she was too good for him..... far too good."

At this point Mr. Baskin rose, "May it please your Lordship, I must enquire, what relevance can these questions possibly have in this case.... I do protest...."

Mr. d'Elgado was quick to interject, "If Milord will allow me to make my point...."

Mr. Justice Humphries was prepared to give him the benefit of his indulgence.

Mr. d'Elgado continued, "Could it perhaps have crossed your mind that this 'attractive, educated lady' could do a lot better than be with the unfortunate Mr. Fisher?"

I said that I did not understand his question.

"Alright, let me put it another way," he snapped, "Were you sexually attracted to the accused?"

Mr. Baskin jumped up again, "Really, Milord, I feel there is no need for this witness to be subjected to an interrogation on his private life."

The Judge waved his hand in a dismissive manner, "For the moment, Mr. Baskin, let it be."

Thus encouraged, the Barrister continued to taunt me, "Come now. You're a single man. You've just told us you find her an attractive woman. Did it not occur to you that she would be doing a lot better with someone like yourself, than the late Mr. Fisher?"

I hoped that the rush of blood to my head would pass unnoticed. I replied evenly, "Absolutely not."

"Did you have any contact whatsoever with her, between your first meeting, when you saw the picture and the fateful evening of August 12th, when the assault took place?"

"I went to a lecture she gave at the ICA."

"Ah, so you went out of your way to meet her again."

"I own a gallery. I attend exhibitions and lectures in London. It's part of my job."

"And after the lecture?"

"We had a drink."

"Ah. You had a drink. And talked about?"

"Commodification."

"Ah yes," he leered, suggestively, "I look at Ms Milford and I think that many a man would like to talk to her... intimately..." he played it for a laugh, "about commodification..."

It was a cheap shot and some members of the jury sniggered.

I said, calmly, "Ms Milford is an expert on the subject."

"So it would appear," he conceded, "It transpires she was running a commodity market in Lowry paintings from her lover's garden shed.

And yet, you knew nothing about this, or so you claim. You see..." he consulted his notes to be reminded of my name, "Mr. Glaser, I find it difficult... I believe the jury will find it difficult, to understand how and why the accused should choose to come to your defence and strike her partner and provider with such force, when you were neither her lover nor her partner in crime..."

I suggested that the accused would be more qualified to answer that question than I.

Mr. d'Elgado ignored this pressed on, "It is my contention that the accused came to your assistance because she was in league with you... that you had formed an attachment..."

Mr. Baskin was on his feet in a flash, "May it please your Lordship.... with respect to my learned friend, I am sure that Milord and the Jury will recognize this absurd assumption as no more than a 'fishing trip', pure and simple, without getting anywhere near a catch. There is no evidence whatsoever to link the accused with this witness, romantically or in any other way."

He turned to me, "And is there any element of truth in the allegation that you were in league with the accused?"

"Absolutely not."

"And that you have developed a relationship with her?"

I replied quietly, "I wish."

There was the suggestion of a restrained titter around the court-room. Patsy smiled at me gratefully. Mr. Baskin thanked me for my evidence.

Mr. Justice Humphrey's summing up, recommended compassion under the tragic circumstances and referred to my evidence as 'compelling proof that Patsy was not in league with me.'

"However," he concluded, "we should not and cannot overlook the fact that the defendant played some part in the fraudulent placing of a fake picture with the bank as security for a loan. She must have had some knowledge that her copy was being used for this purpose."

I spent two agonizing hours waiting for the Jury to return with its verdict....

CHAPTER 46

It has been a lonely but rewarding business, committing my notes and memories to paper, completing the story we started together. It brings me closer to Nathan. I see him visibly before me: both of us in uniform at Nüremburg forty years ago. I recall his challenge as though it were yesterday: 'you can have my story, but I want 50% of the royalties.' I mumble to myself: 'you shall have it Nathan. You shall have it the moment the book gets published, I promise you.'

My inspiration comes with what I see before me as I write. I spend much time just looking at it and if I allow myself to dwell on the story of its acquisition, I am constantly reminded of poor Nathan and how his passion for Lowrys cost him his life.

Shops and People in Salford is quite the star of my collection and dominates the room. With its sharpness of colour, its three-dimensional aspect, smoking chimneys and impasto sky, it mesmerises me. I cannot be in the room without being drawn to look at the figures as they hurry about, without imaging the scenes and dialogue in the shops, houses and factories.

She did make a wonderful job of it, almost as good as the original hanging beside it. I have to admit, I'm hooked on her art-form. It may not be creative in the sense of original, but the complex mix of skills required to make a convincing duplicate – the grasp of technique, colour matching, knowledge of pigment chemistry – commands my respect. Perhaps even more than does the artist spontaneously committing his vision to canvas. As I cease-lessly focus from original to copy and back again, can I honestly claim that the one affords less visual pleasure than the other? Prestige, of course and pride of ownership play their part. But I view the two pictures with equal delight. Could it be that Patsy's skills might allow the genuine Lowry lover a chance to enjoy the genius of his creation?

I have visited her several times in Holloway, trying to support her a little through her two-year sentence. With one year's remission, probable, she is remarkably optimistic and accepts her fate as a 'dark night of the soul'. With each visit, I feel a stronger bond of friendship. I count the days from one visit to the next. We joke about Mr. D'Elgado's prophetic interrogation.

She tells me her legal team is doing well. Carl Fisher died intestate. They are claiming ownership of the Hartlepool house on her behalf, as Carl's common law wife. They expect to succeed.

"Not that I could ever bear to live there again," she says, "Or even go near the place. But it would enable me to buy somewhere suitable for Georgina and I to live near London."

I am pleased to hear that news.

Lately, my visits have become more regular and laid the foundation for a personal relationship. I think of little else. Last week, she put her hand over mine and asked if I would do her a great favour. She hasn't seen Georgina, wanting to shield her from the sight of her mother in jail. Georgina is staying with Patsy's brother and despised sister-in-law in Godalming. Patsy asks me to visit them and spend a little time with Georgina to see how she's getting on. "We write to each other of course, but it would be wonderful to get a first hand account of how she looks and what she's doing..."

I am flattered at being pulled into the family circle and tell her I will go with pleasure and bring back a full report.

She sheds an emotional tear as she talks about her daughter. I comfort her. Even in distress, she looks radiant. I say, "When you come out of this place, I'm going to commission you to paint some Lowry's. Just for me." I chuckle, "But remember, you must paint the canvas white and bake it. That's the secret to a Lowry. Then, no one will ever know."

She kisses me and promises she will.

As I leave, I walk on air. My love for her knows no boundaries.

Today, It is the anniversary of Nathan's death. I light a candle in memory of my murdered friend. I tell him that I have done all that I promised all those years ago. I have set down in writing his story and my own.

An important event in my life approaches. Patsy is to be released

195

from prison and I have promised to help her resettle. I am to collect her tonight and we will celebrate her freedom together. I feel it is the start of a new life.

I pray my dear friend Nathan, that you might not disapprove.